Te...
Read Music for Guitar

DAN FOX

Alfred Music Publishing Co., Inc.
P.O. Box 10003
Van Nuys, CA 91410-0003
alfred.com

ISBN-10: 0-7390-3779-X (Book & CD)
ISBN-13: 978-0-7390-3779-9 (Book & CD)

Cover photos: Martin acoustic guitar courtesy of Martin Guitar Company.
Daisy Rock Stardust Elite guitar courtesy of Daisy Rock Guitars.

PREFACE

This book starts from the very beginning. It takes you through all the most-used keys on the guitar, the positions from first to seventh, and various rhythms including intermediate to advanced syncopations (the basis of jazz, rock, Latin, and virtually all popular styles). It even illustrates odd meters such as $\frac{5}{4}$ and $\frac{7}{8}$.

If you go through the book carefully, you will be able to play lead sheets and easy to moderately difficult stage band arrangements at sight. This will give you a distinct advantage over those who must memorize everything they want to play by listening to recordings or other players over and over again.

Also, if you aspire to do any kind of studio work—recordings, movie scores, and the like—being a top-notch reader is an absolute necessity. This is the book that will give you a firm basis on which to start your career.

INTRODUCING WRITTEN MUSIC

The two most important things you can learn from written music are *pitch* (how high or low a note is) and *duration* (how long or short a note is). There are other refinements such as *dynamics* (how loud or soft the note is) and *tempo* (how fast the piece should be played), but pitch and duration are enough to start performing music at sight.

All music in traditional notation is written on a five-line *staff*.

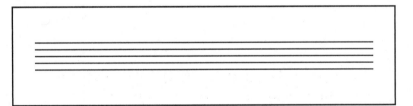

Virtually all music has an underlying steady pulse called the *beat*. In some music such as marches, rock, hip-hop, country, or jazz, the beat is easy to hear. It's what you tap your foot to. In some classical music and ethnic styles, the beat is more subtle, but it's always there.

In written music, the shape of a note tells you its *duration*, meaning how many beats (or parts of beats) it lasts. Notes are written as either an open oval o, an oval with a stem ♩♪, a solid black note with a stem ♩♪, or a solid black note with a stem and flag ♪♪. Shorter notes are indicated by adding more flags to the stem (♪♪).

Longer notes ⟶ Shorter notes

Every note has an equivalent *rest*. Rests are used when silence is called for. It is important to remember that rests are **measured silences**; they last for a certain number of beats.

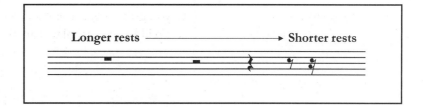

A note can be placed on a line or in a space. The higher the note is on the staff, the higher the pitch; the lower the note is on the staff, the lower the pitch.

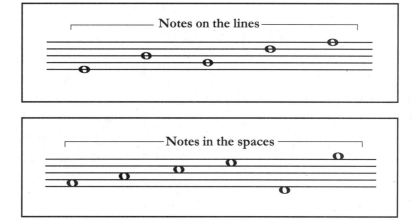

Music notation uses the letters A, B, C, D, E, F, and G. In order to identify the lines and spaces on the staff, a *clef* is used. The two most common clefs are the *treble clef* and the *bass clef*. The treble clef, sometimes called the *G clef*, is derived from the Gothic letter "G"; it curls around the second staff line, which is the note G. The bass clef, sometimes called the *F clef*, is derived from the Gothic letter "F"; the two dots straddle the fourth line of the staff, which is the note F.

Music for the guitar is written in the treble clef on the standard five-line staff.

In order to make music easier to read and to show the basic rhythmic pulse, *bar lines* separate music into *measures* (sometimes called *bars*).

A double thin bar line marks the end of a section; a thin/thick *double bar line* marks the end of a piece.

If fingering is used, small numbers are placed near or over the notes to which they apply. The numbers refer to the left hand: 1=index; 2=middle; 3=ring; 4=pinky.
A small ○ means "open string" (no fingers used).

For *pickstyle* playing (also called *flat-picking*), this sign ⊓ above a note means to *down-pick*; this sign V means to *up-pick*.

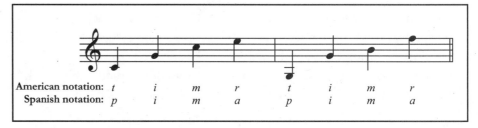

For *fingerstyle* playing, some music for guitar contains letters to indicate the fingers of the right hand:

> *t*=**thumb,**   *i*=**index,**
> *m*=**middle,**   *r*=**ring.**

Often, especially in classical guitar music, letters that refer to the Spanish names of the fingers are used:

> *p*=**thumb,**   *i*=**index,**
> *m*=**middle,**   *a*=**ring.**

The right-hand pinky is not used in fingerstyle playing.

Using a Metronome

A metronome is a device that produces a steady stream of clicks that are evenly spaced. The speed of the clicks can be as slow as 40 beats per minute or as fast as 208 beats per minute. Nowadays metronomes are electronic, and a reliable one can be purchased for as little as $20.00. Some metronomes can also be set to accent each 2nd, 3rd, 4th, 5th, or 6th click. Others can produce an electronic tone that sounds the note A to help you keep your guitar in tune. We highly recommend the use of a metronome which will help you keep a steady beat. And by setting the speed a little faster each day, it will enable you to monitor your progress.

QUARTER NOTES & QUARTER RESTS

1. Set your metronome to 96, or tap your foot to a steady beat.
2. Pick the open high E string once for each beat.

 ## Quarter Notes

These notes are called *quarter notes*.  The stem may go either up or down.

Foot
Taps: tap   tap   tap   tap   tap   etc.

 ## Time Signatures

So you can tell how many beats are in each measure, a symbol called a *time signature* is placed directly after the clef. The top number tells you how many beats are in each measure.

The bottom number tells you what kind of note gets one beat. In all these examples, a quarter note gets one beat.

The top number in the $\frac{4}{4}$ time signature tells you that the beats occur in groups of four.
This is called $\frac{4}{4}$ (say "four-four" or "four-quarter") time.

Count: 1   2   3   4   1   2   3   4   1   2   3   4   1   2   3   4

The top number in the $\frac{3}{4}$ time signature tells you that the beats occur in groups of three.
This is called $\frac{3}{4}$ (say "three-four" or "three-quarter") time.

Count: 1   2   3   1   2   3   1   2   3   1   2   3

The top number in the $\frac{2}{4}$ time signature tells you that the beats occur in groups of two.
This is called $\frac{2}{4}$ (say "two-four" or "two-quarter") time.

Count: 1   2   1   2   1   2   1   2

 ## Quarter Rests

This symbol 𝄽 is a *quarter rest*, and it stands for one beat of silence.
For a rest, muffle the string with the heel of the right hand.

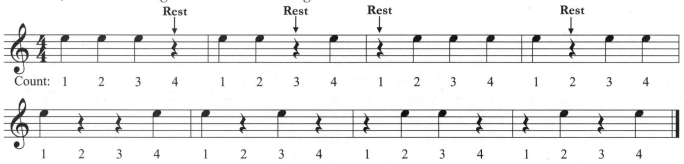

Count: 1   2   3   4   1   2   3   4   1   2   3   4   1   2   3   4

        1   2   3   4   1   2   3   4   1   2   3   4   1   2   3   4

Notes on the E or 1st String

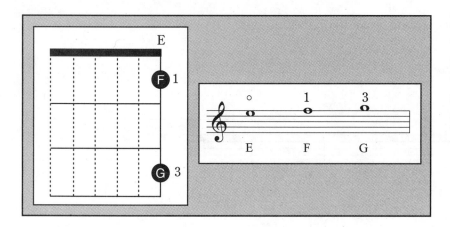

In first position, there are three diatonic notes on the 1st string, the high E string. (The word *diatonic* means natural notes without sharps or flats, like the white keys on a piano.) E is played on the open string; F is played with the 1st finger at the 1st fret; G is played with the 3rd finger at the 3rd fret.

Here are some exercises that combine E, F, and G with some rhythms you already learned.
Suggested metronome setting: 80

Notes on the 1st String, the E String

Notes on the 1st String in 4/4

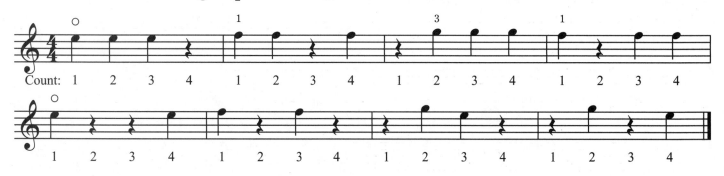

Notes on the 1st String in 3/4

Notes on the 1st String in 2/4

HALF NOTES & HALF RESTS

 These notes are *half notes.* ♩ ♪ They last twice as long as quarter notes, with a duration of two beats.

Play the following examples of half notes in ⁴⁄₄ and ²⁄₄ time.

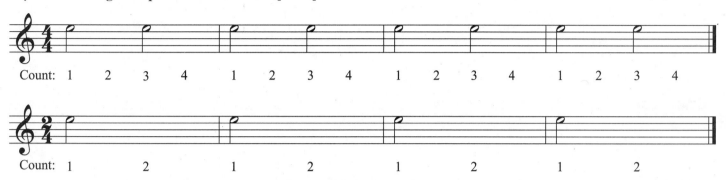

Often, half notes are combined with quarter notes and rests.

 A *half rest* looks like a heavy dash resting on the third staff line. It gets two beats.

This rest only occurs on the first or third beat in ⁴⁄₄ time. When a two-beat rest occurs in the middle of a ⁴⁄₄ measure, as in measure 7 below, two quarter rests are used.

Once you are secure with the rhythms on this page, you can play the examples on the next page.

READING MUSIC ON THE 1ST STRING

 MINI MUSIC LESSON The abbreviation MM means to set your metronome to a particular speed.

Strolling in 4/4 Time
Goal: MM=104

Little Waltz
Goal: MM=144

Little March
Goal: MM=126

Notes on the B or 2nd String

In the first position, there are three diatonic notes on the 2nd string, the B string: B is played on the open string; C is played with the 1st finger at the 1st fret; D is played with the 3rd finger at the 3rd fret.

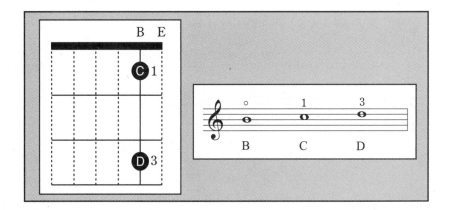

Notes on the 2nd String, the B String

Notes on the 1st and 2nd Strings

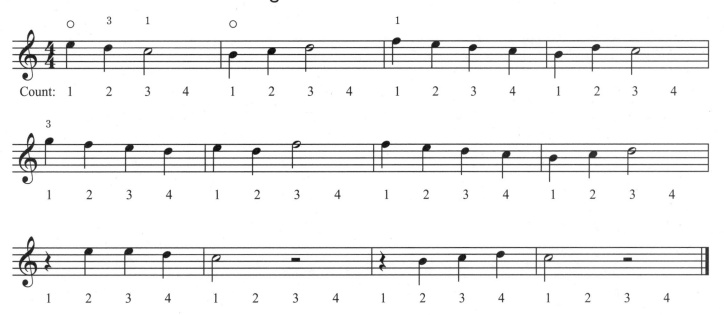

Note: Resist the temptation to write in the names of the notes. Although it will seem easier at first, later it will stand in the way of your ability to read music fluently.

WHOLE NOTES & WHOLE RESTS

 A *whole note* looks like this: o

As you can see, a whole note doesn't have a stem. It gets four beats, and because of this, can only occur in $\frac{4}{4}$ time.

Count: 1   2   3   4   1   2   3   4   1   2   3   4   1   2   3   4

 The *whole rest* looks like a heavy dash hanging from the fourth staff line.
Unlike every other rhythmic symbol in music, whole rests do not have a fixed number of beats.

In $\frac{4}{4}$ time, whole rests get four beats.

Count: 1   2   3   4   1   2   3   4   1   2   3   4   1   2   3   4

In $\frac{3}{4}$ time, whole rests get three beats.

Count: 1   2   3   1   2   3   1   2   3   1   2   3

In $\frac{2}{4}$ time, whole rests get two beats.

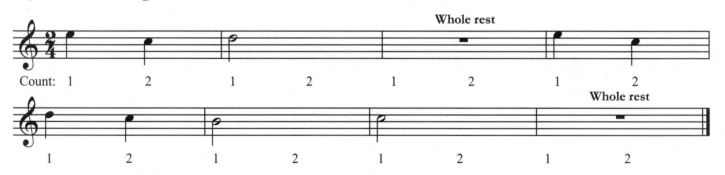

Count: 1   2   1   2   1   2   1   2

1   2   1   2   1   2   1   2

Merrily We Roll Along

1   2   3   4

Notes on the G or 3rd String

In the first position, there are two diatonic notes on the 3rd string, the G string: G is played on the open string; A is played with the 2nd finger at the 2nd fret.

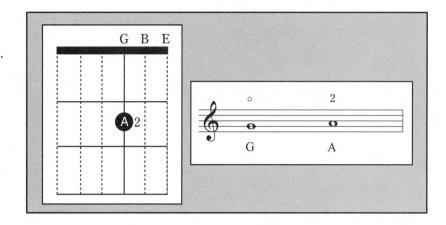

Notes on the G String, the 3rd String

Notes on the 2nd & 3rd Strings

MINI MUSIC LESSON The abbreviation **C** means the same thing as $\frac{4}{4}$ time.

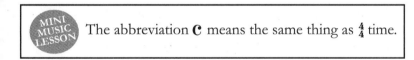

London Bridge

English children's song

THE DOTTED HALF NOTE

Placing a dot after a note increases its value by half. Ordinarily, a half note gets two beats; with a dot after it, it gets three beats and is called a *dotted half note.*

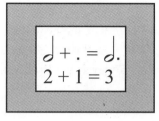

Big Ben Chimes

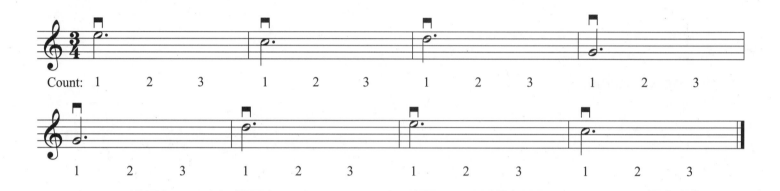

Jacob's Ladder

The dotted half note can appear in $\frac{4}{4}$ time, but not in $\frac{2}{4}$.

African-American spiritual

SHARPS, NATURALS, AND THE G MAJOR SCALE

Sharps

This sign ♯ is called a *sharp*. Placing a sharp before a note means to play that note one fret higher than the unaltered note. For example, F is played on the 1st string, 1st fret; F♯ is played on the 1st string, 2nd fret.

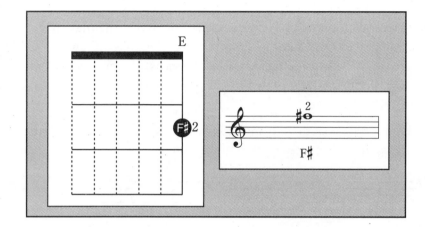

The sharp applies to the note it precedes as well as other notes of that pitch in the same measure.

Naturals

This sign ♮ is called a *natural*. It restores a sharp note to its original pitch. If a natural note follows a sharp note in the same measure, the natural sign is used.

The G Major Scale

The *major scale* is very important because it is used in music to construct melodies and build chords. The *G major scale* begins and ends on G and consists of the notes G A B C D E F♯.

KEYS AND KEY SIGNATURES

Every piece of music in this book is written in one of many possible *keys*. A key is a sort of musical "home base" to which the melody usually returns. If a piece is in the *key of C*, most of the notes in the melody will belong to the *C scale*, which consists of the notes C D E F G A B. The last note of the melody will also probably be C, which gives a sense of completion and finality.

Here is a typical short melody in the key of C. Notice that every note belongs to the C scale (C D E F G A B), and that the melody comes to rest on the note C.

Here's a short tune in the *key of G*. All the notes belong to the G scale (see p. 13), and the melody finishes on the note G.

THE KEY OF G MAJOR

Notice that in the above example in the key of G, every time the note F appears, it is written as an F♯. In order to save the trouble of writing in all those F♯s, a *key signature* of one sharp is placed on the F line of the staff. This means that every F in the piece is played as F♯.

The following short tune is played exactly like the one above.

If a natural F note is called for, a natural sign is placed in front of it.

Using the key signature of one sharp, the G major scale can be written like this:

TIES

Two or more notes of the same pitch may be joined together with a *tie*. When two notes are tied, the second one is not played separately. Simply add the number of beats together.

Hold for 5 beats.

Ties in 3/4

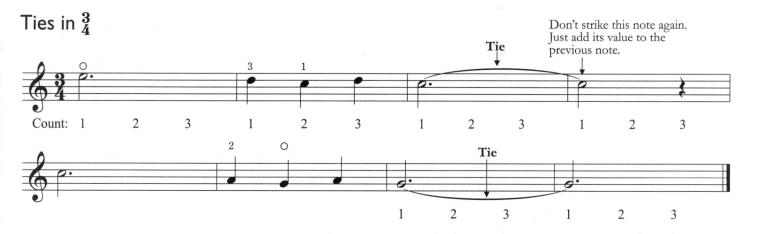

Ties in Common Time

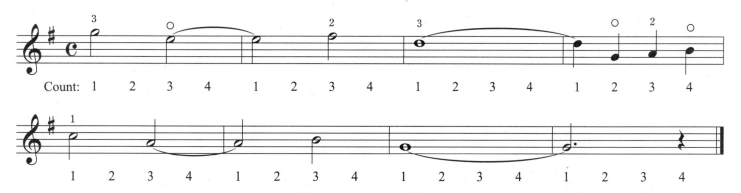

Ties in 2/4

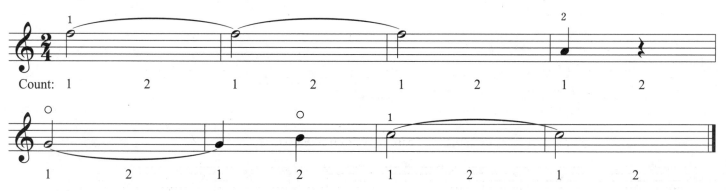

 **PICKUPS**

Sometimes a song or other piece of music begins with an incomplete measure called a *pickup*. In $\frac{4}{4}$ time, the pickup can be one, two, or three beats. (Later you'll learn that pickups can also use parts of a beat.) Often, but not always, the final measure will be missing the beats that the pickup uses. For example, if there's a one-beat pickup in $\frac{4}{4}$, the last measure may have only three beats.

Here are some short excerpts of familiar tunes showing various numbers of beats in $\frac{4}{4}$ and $\frac{3}{4}$ time.

Jimmy Crack Corn

A one-beat pickup in $\frac{4}{4}$ time. Notice the last measure has only three beats.

Count: (1)(2)(3) 4   1   2   3
          When I   was young I   used to wait on   mas - ter and give him his plate

Red River Valley

A two-beat pickup in $\frac{4}{4}$. Notice that the last measure has only two beats.

Count: (1) (2)   3   4   1   2
        From this val - ley they   say   you   are   go - ing_____

Oh Happy Day

A three-beat pickup in $\frac{4}{4}$. The last measure has only one beat.

Count: (1)   2   3   4   1
           Oh hap - py   day_____ that fixed my   choice_____

The Beautiful Blue Danube

A one-beat pickup in $\frac{3}{4}$. The last measure has only two beats.

Count: (1) (2) 3   1   2

Cowboy Jack

A two-beat pickup in $\frac{3}{4}$. The last measure has only one beat.
Remember that all F's are sharp because of the key signature.

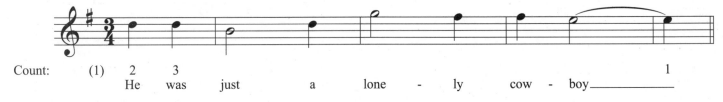

Count: (1)   2   3   1
            He   was just   a   lone - ly   cow - boy_____

 CHORDS

One of the things that the guitar does best is *chords*. A chord is a group of three or more notes that sound good together. Mostly you'll see chords referred to by symbols such as G, D7, Am, and so on.

Each of these symbols names a chord that has at least three notes in it, but may have as many as six on the guitar.

When written out in standard notation, the notes of the chords are placed on one stem. Here are some three-string chords in standard notation:

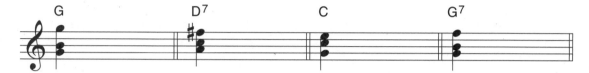

Often, however, *chord diagrams*, also called *chord frames*, are used to describe a chord. These contain six vertical lines that represent the six strings of the guitar. They also have four or five horizontal lines that represent the frets.

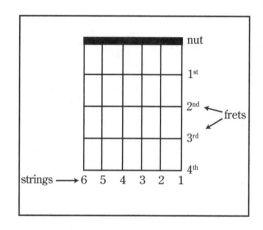

The position of the fingers is indicated by numbered circles on the strings. Open strings are shown by an o; strings that are not used are shown with an ×.

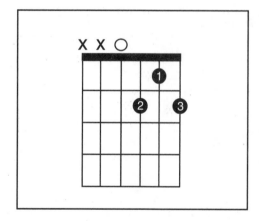

Here are some diagrams for the chords used on the next page. Notice that the diagrams can call for notes you haven't learned yet.

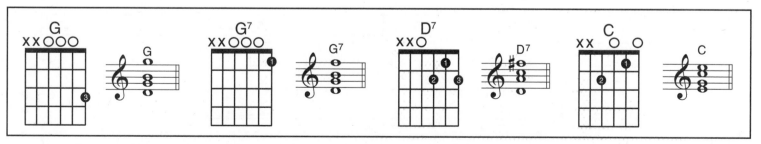

Since this is basically a book about reading music, we won't spend a lot of time with chords; however, playing chords is a very important part of guitar playing, so we recommend studying them with a book such as Alfred's *Guitar Chord Encyclopedia* (item 4432).

CHORD SYMBOLS

From now on in this book, every song or other complete piece will have *chord symbols* above the staff. These will allow another guitar or chordal instrument to play an accompaniment while you play the written melody.

When the Saints Go Marching In

Dixieland jazz standard

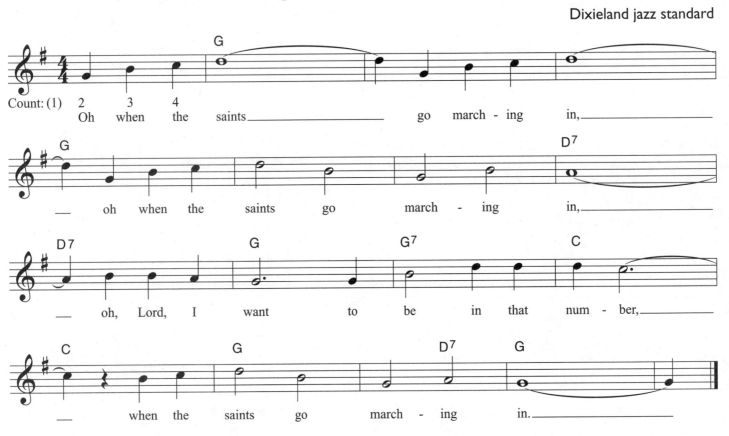

Down in the Valley

American folk song

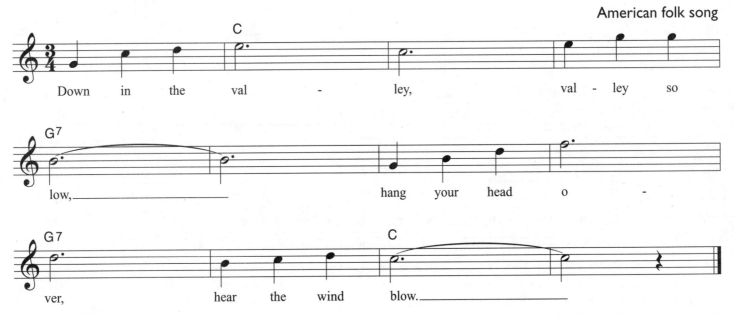

EIGHTH NOTES

These notes are *eighth notes*. ♪♪ When written in groups of two or four, they look like this:

Eighth notes are played twice as fast as quarter notes, that is, two for each beat.

In $\frac{4}{4}$, count them as 1 & 2 & 3 & 4 &.

In $\frac{3}{4}$, count 1 & 2 & 3 &. When playing pickstyle guitar, pairs of eighth notes are usually played with downstrokes and upstrokes. Fingerstyle players use alternating index and middle fingers.

Make sure you can play the first line accurately before attempting the rest of the page.

Eighth Notes in $\frac{3}{4}$ Time

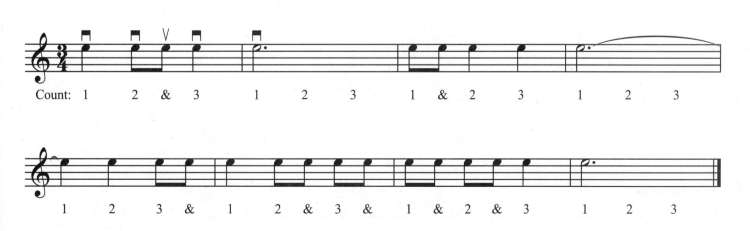

Can-Can (from Orpheus in the Underworld)

Jacques Offenbach

Pick a Bale o' Cotton

American folk song

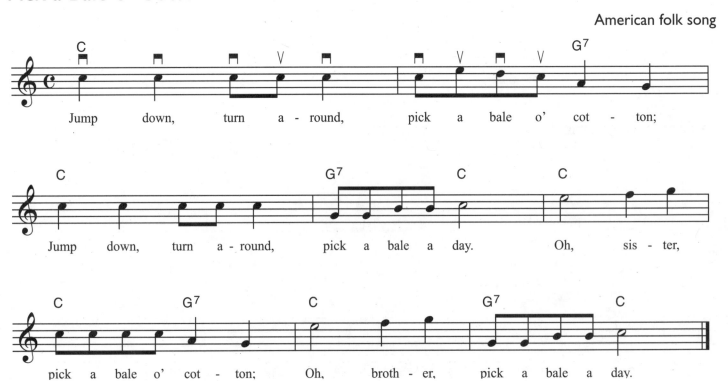

Jump down, turn a - round, pick a bale o' cot - ton;

Jump down, turn a - round, pick a bale a day. Oh, sis - ter,

pick a bale o' cot - ton; Oh, broth - er, pick a bale a day.

Notes on the D or 4th String

In first position, three diatonic notes can be played on the 4th string, the D string: D is the open string, E is played with the 2nd finger at the 2nd fret; E is played with the 3rd finger at the 3rd fret. Since a sharp raises a note by one fret, the F♯ on the 4th string is played with the 4th finger at the 4th fret.

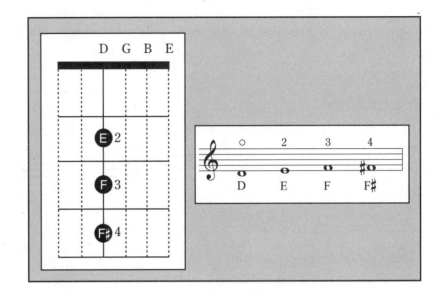

The following exercises make use of the notes on the 4th string.

Using F♯ and F♮

Note: The natural here is not really needed but is often included as a "courtesy" or reminder.

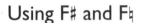

Notes on the 3rd and 4th Strings

Notes on the First Four Strings

Remember: In the key of G, **all** F's are sharp, including the F on the 4th string.

THE KEY OF D MAJOR

The *D major scale* requires two notes, F and C, to be always played sharp. C♯ on the 2nd string is played one fret higher than C, with the 2nd finger at the 2nd fret.

First practice the scale, making sure to play all the F's and C's as F♯'s and C♯'s. Then play the two melodies in the key of D. Notice the key signature.

D Major Scale

Little Brown Jug Polka

Traditional

Brother John (Frère Jacques)

French round

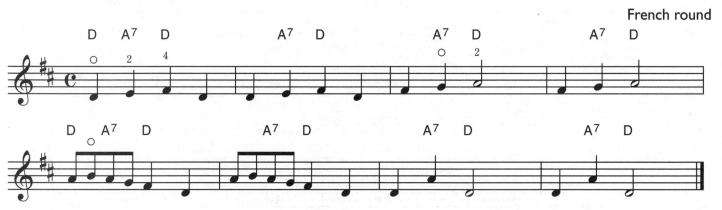

SHARPS IN FIRST POSITION

As you already know, a sharp raises the pitch of a note one fret.
The distance of one fret is called a *half step*.

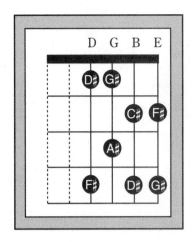

Here are all the sharp notes in first position on the first four strings.

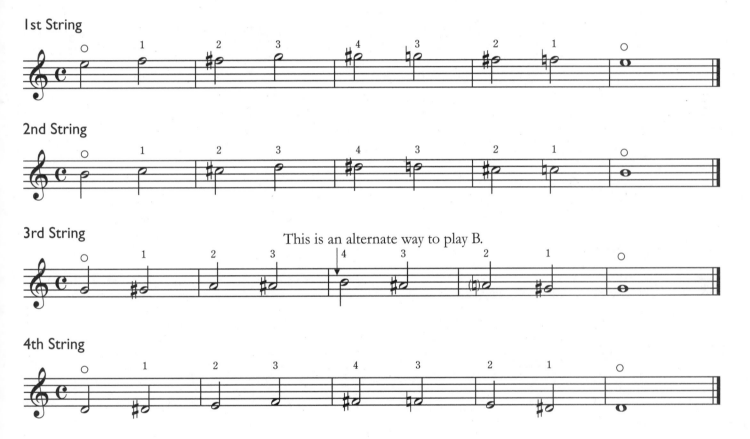

Old Joe Clarke

Remember that after a sharp note, every note of that pitch in the same measure is also sharp.

American square dance tune

Rockin' the Bach

Adapted from a minuet by J.S. Bach

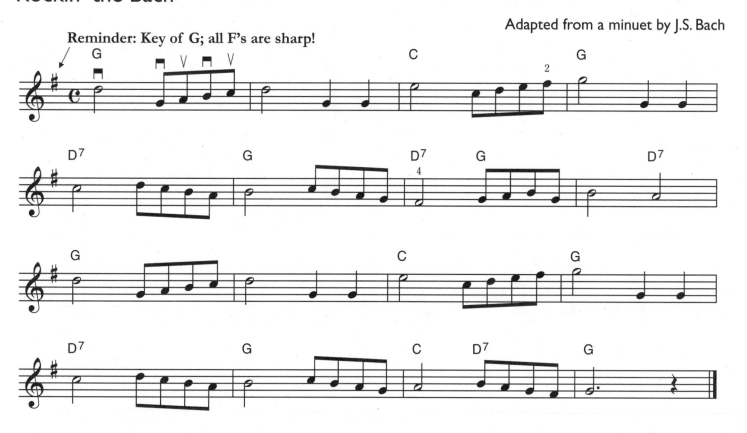

Canon (Main Theme)

Johann Pachelbel

Notes on the A or 5th String

In first position, three diatonic notes can be played on the 5th string, the A string: A is the open string; B is played with the 2nd finger at the 2nd fret; C is played with the 3rd finger at the 3rd fret. There are also two sharp notes: A♯ is played with the 1st finger at the 1st fret; C♯ is played with the 4th finger at the 4th fret.

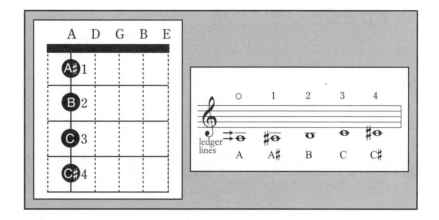

Notes on the A String, the 5th String

Because these notes on the A string lie below the five-line staff,
they are written using a short, temporary extension of the staff called a *ledger line*.

Waltz in A

Rockin' with Henry

Use all downpicks to get a more hard-driving sound.

THE KEY OF C MAJOR

C Major Scale

As you know, the C major scale has no sharps.

 Music that is based on the C major scale has nothing in the key signature, and is said to be in the *key of C major.*

Exercise in C Major

Reuben, Reuben

This sign ⌢ is called a *fermata* (or "bird's eye"). It means to hold the note about half again as long as usual. For example, a half note with a fermata is held for about three beats.

Early Vaudeville song

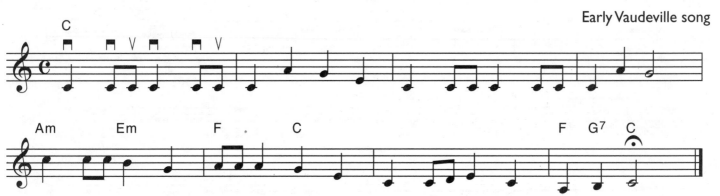

Vieni sul Mar (Come to the Sea)

Reminder: Key of D; F and C are played as F♯ and C♯.

Neapolitan folk song

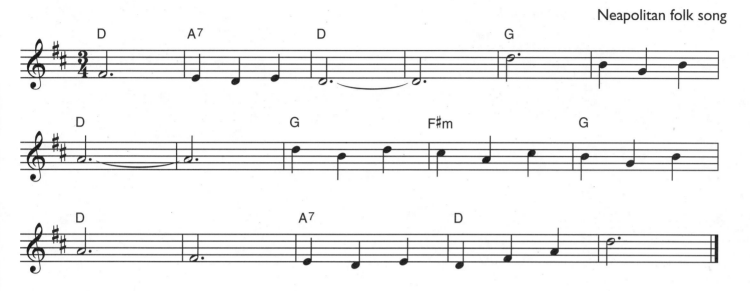

Ah! Marie

Reminder: Two-beat pickup in ¾ time; last measure has only one beat.

Eduardo di Capra

 **THE FLAT**

The *flat* symbol ♭ is used to indicate that a note should be played one fret lower (closer to the nut). For example, high G is played on the 1st string, 3rd fret; G♭ is played on the 1st string, 2nd fret.

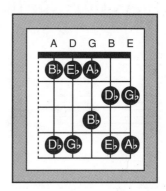

Here are the flats on the first five strings in first position.

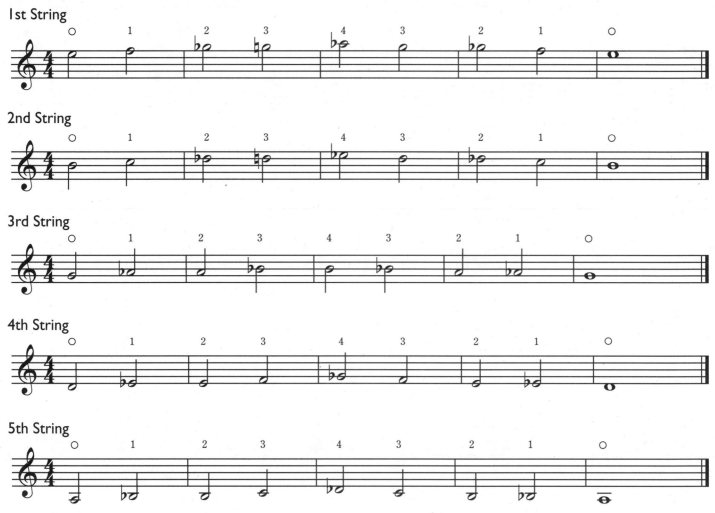

 Flats, like sharps, affect every note of the same pitch that follows the flatted note in that particular measure. If the unaltered note is called for, a natural is used.

Although the bar line cancels any *accidental* (a flat, sharp, or natural), sometimes a courtesy accidental is used after the bar line as a reminder to the player.

My Melancholy Baby

George Norton and Ernie Burnett

THE KEY OF F MAJOR

The *F major scale* requires the note B to be always played as B♭.
Notice the key signature of one flat.

F Major Scale

Scale Study in F Major

On Top of Old Smoky

American folk song

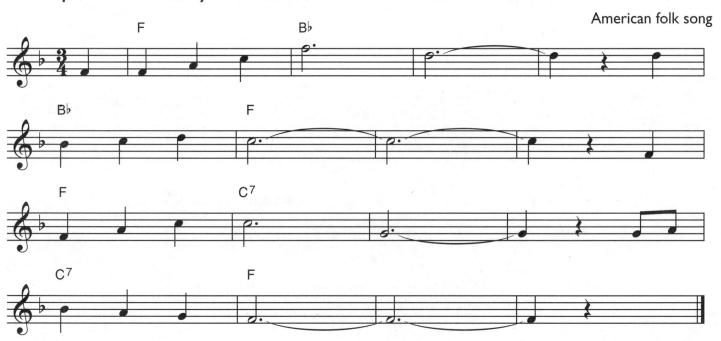

ENHARMONICS

In "Getting' Down with Sweet Genevieve," you'll notice that certain notes can be named with either a sharp or a flat. These are called *enharmonics*. The five most common enharmonics are C♯ & D♭, D♯ & E♭, F♯ & G♭, G♯ & A♭, A♯ & B♭. If you know a little about keyboards, you'll realize that these pairs of notes represent the five black keys in each octave. Why do you need to know this? Let's say you're looking for a low D♭. The rule for flatting a note is to move it one fret lower, but this can't be done with the open D string; so instead of looking for low D♭, look for the same note with a different name, in this case, C♯, found on the 5th string, 4th fret. Since we know that C♯ and D♭ are the same note, we have solved the problem of finding low D♭, also on the 5th string, 4th fret.

See the fingerboard chart on page 112 for the location of every sharp, flat, and natural note in the first position.

Gettin' Down with Sweet Genevieve

Reminder: Key of F major; all B's are played as B♭'s, unless preceded by a natural sign.

DOTTED QUARTER NOTES

As you already know, placing a dot after a note increases its time value by half. That's why a dotted half note gets three beats: a half note with 2 beats, plus 1 beat (half of 2 beats), equals 3 beats.

A dot after a quarter note increases the quarter note value by half. Half a quarter note is equal to an eighth note; therefore, a dotted quarter note is the same as a quarter note tied to an eighth note.

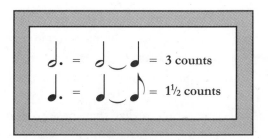

The second line is played exactly the same as the first line

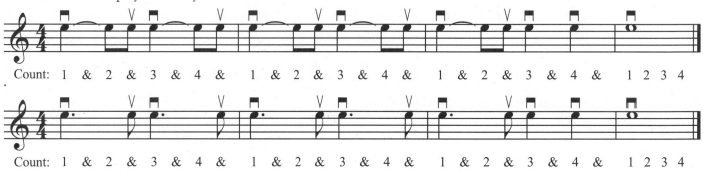

All Through the Night

The dotted quarter/eighth note rhythm is often used melodically, as in this famous tune.

Welsh Christmas carol

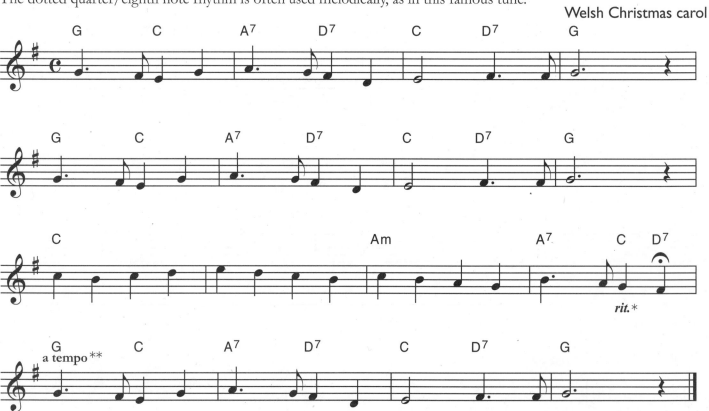

*The abbreviation *rit.* stands for the Italian word *ritardando*, which means "slowing down."
**The Italian words *a tempo* mean "resume normal tempo."

Get Down

The dotted quarter/eighth note rhythm can also be used in a more rhythmic context,
as in this typical rock figure from the 1950s and '60s.

**Use B on the
3rd string, 4th fret**

Oh Susanna!

Here is another example of the melodic use of the dotted quarter/eighth note figure.

Stephen Foster

Notes on the Low E or 6th String

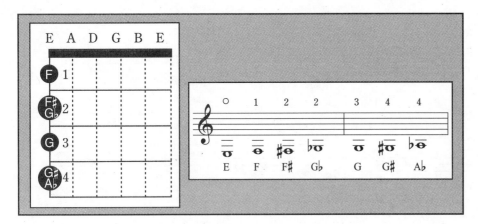

In the first position, three diatonic notes can be played on the 6th string, the low E string: low E is the open string; F is played with the 1st finger at the 1st fret; G is played with the 3rd finger at the 3rd fret. Two other notes can also be played: F♯ or G♭ is played with the 2nd finger at the 2nd fret; G♯ or A♭ is played with the 4th finger at the 4th fret.

Diatonic Notes on the Low E String

Sharps and Naturals

Flats and Naturals

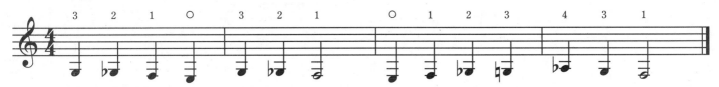

Sharps, Flats, and Naturals

TWO-OCTAVE MAJOR SCALES

The word *octave* is used to describe a span of eight notes (such as C to C, G to G, etc.). For example, a one-octave C major scale consists of the eight notes C D E F G A B C.

A two-octave scale consists of 15 notes (not 16, because the eighth note of the scale is common to both octaves).

Two-Octave F Major Scale

The Yellow Rose of Texas

American folk song

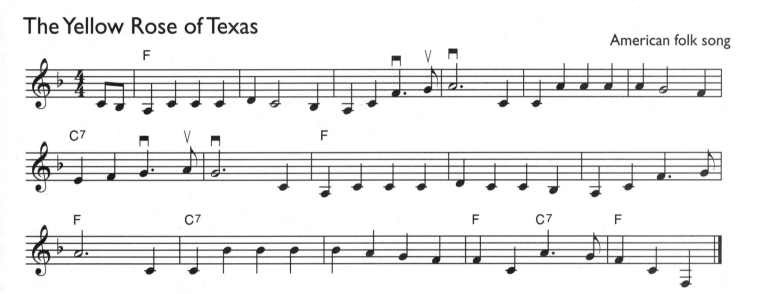

Two-Octave G Major Scale

Rock with Two Octaves

 EIGHTH RESTS

This symbol ♩ is an *eighth rest*, and it stands for a half beat of silence.
Eighth rests can occur on the "&," which is called the *upbeat*. Count carefully.

When a rest follows a fingered note, as in the line below,
release the pressure of the finger to create the silence.

When a rest follows an open note, stop the vibration
of the string with the heel of the right hand.

Eighth rests are often seen in 2/4 time,
as in this example of a country-style bass line.

When an eighth rest occurs *on* the beat (the *downbeat*),
it can be helpful to mark the silence with a foot tap.

Don't forget to tap your foot for all down-beat eighth rests.

High A on the 1st String

The staff can be extended upward by the use of ledger lines. The note that is written one ledger line above the staff is called *high A*. It is played at the 5th fret, usually with the 4th finger. Here are all the notes that can be played on the high E string in first position.

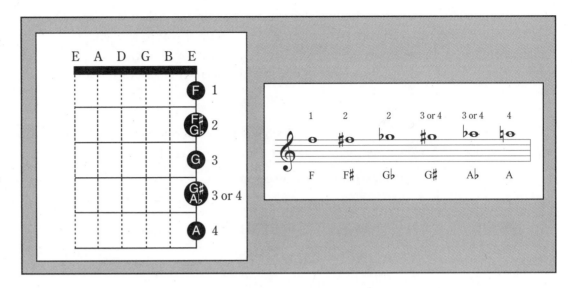

The following exercise will give you a workout on the high E string.

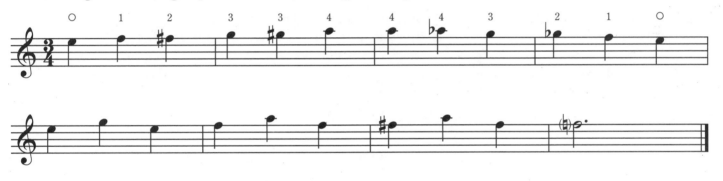

Shortnin' Bread

African-American folk song

DYNAMICS

Music notation as we know it today made its greatest strides in 17th-century Europe. At that time, Italians dominated the music scene, and for that reason, many of the expressions we use in music are in the Italian language. *Dynamics* indicate how loud or soft to play and are based on three Italian words: *piano* means soft, *forte* means loud, and *mezzo* means medium or moderately.

A dynamic mark applies to the note under which it is placed and to every succeeding note until a new dynamic mark is reached. The most commonly used dynamics are as follows:

pp	*pianissimo* (pyan-NEES-see-moh)	very soft
p	*piano* (PYAH-noh)	soft
mp	*mezzo-piano* (MED-zoh PYAH-noh)	moderately soft
mf	*mezzo-forte* (MED-zoh FOHR-teh)	moderately loud
f	*forte* (FOHR-teh)	loud
ff	*fortissimo* (fohr-TEES-see-moh)	very loud

Occasionally, you may see dynamics even softer than *pp*, such as *ppp*, which means *pianississimo* (pyah-nees-SEES-see-moh), or louder than *ff*, such as *fff*, which means *fortississimo* (fohr-tees-SEES-see-moh).

Also commonly used is a temporary change in dynamic such as *sfz*, *sforzando* (sfor-TSAHN-doh), which means to become suddenly loud for one note only and then go back to the previous dynamic.

Also important are the effects of gradually getting louder or softer. These are also Italian words.

crescendo (kreh-SHEN-doh), abbreviated **cresc.**	gradually getting louder
decrescendo (deh-kreh-SHEN-doh), abbreviated **decresc.**	gradually getting softer
diminuendo (dee-mee-noo-EN-doh), abbreviated **dim.**	gradually getting softer

Another way of notating these is by using long, wedge-shaped marks familiarly known as "hairpins."

      ◁   getting louder

      ▷   getting softer

On the guitar, dynamics are produced by how hard you strike the string. The harder you strike, the louder the tone.

The proper use of dynamics is one of the things that distinguishes an artistic player from an amateur.
Get in the habit of paying attention to the dynamics and playing them accurately.

Dynamics in Action

Stepping Lightly

Sippin' Cider Through a Straw

American folk song

THE EIGHTH-NOTE TRIPLET

An *eighth-note triplet* is a group of three eighth notes played in one beat. This means that each note of the triplet is played a little faster than an ordinary eighth note.

You'll recognize the triplet by the number 3 over or under the three eighth notes. First practice the exercises, then play the song.

Count: 1 2 trip-let 3 4 trip-let 1 2 trip-let 3 4 trip-let 1 2 trip-let 3 4 trip-let 1 2 3 4

Triplets in ¾ Time

Eighth Notes and Eighth-Note Triplets

Be careful not to rush the triplets!

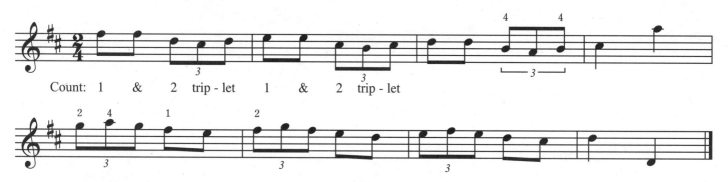

Count: 1 & 2 trip - let 1 & 2 trip - let

Amazing Grace

American folk hymn

ARTICULATIONS

Articulations are marks placed above or below a note that help you play with the right expression.

 > An *accent* means to play the note a little louder than the notes surrounding it.

Make sure to contrast the unaccented line with the accented one.

 · A *staccato* dot means to cut the note off short.
The two lines below are played nearly the same.

 — A *tenuto* dash means to stress the note slightly and hold it for its full time value.

Articulation marks can also be combined on the same note.

Articulations and dynamics are two important ways to give your music reading professional polish.

SIXTEENTH NOTES

These notes are *sixteenth notes*. They are often seen in groups of four. Sixteenth notes are played four to a beat. They are twice as fast as eighth notes and four times as fast as quarter notes.

Practice these two lines on the open E string. Count carefully. If playing pickstyle, use down and up picks. For fingerstyle, use index and middle fingers.

Count: 1 e & a 2 e & a 3 e & a 4 e & a   1 e & a 2 e & a 3 e & a 4 e & a   1 e & a 2 e & a 3 e & a 4 e & a   1 2 3 4

Count: 1   2   3   4   1 & 2 & 3 & 4 &   1 e & a 2 e & a 3 e & a 4 e & a   1 2 3 4

Sixteenth Notes on Open Strings

Count: 1 e & a 2   3 e & a 4

Melody in G

Melody in C

Sixteenth Notes in ¾ Time

Melody in D

Rakes of Mallow (Part 1)

An eighth note followed by two sixteenths is a commonly seen figure, especially in music with a bright, spirited feel. These two lines teach this rhythm on open strings. After you master them, try the melodies that follow.

Count: 1   & a 2   & a 1   & a 2   & a 1   & a 2   & a 1   & 2

The Drunken Sailor (Melody and Variation)

Sea chantey

Rakes of Mallow (Part 2)

Irish tune

A rhythmic figure consisting of two sixteenth notes followed by an eighth note is also fairly common.
Make sure you can play these first two lines before attempting the songs.

Count: 1   e   &   2   e   &   1   e   &   2   e   &   1   e   &   2   e   &   1   &   2   &

Someone's in the Kitchen with Dinah (Melody and Variation)

Minstrel show tune

Reuben and Rachel (Melody and Variation)

Minstrel show tune

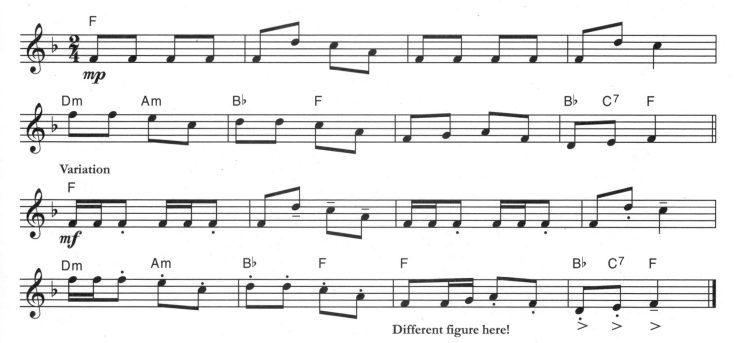

Different figure here!

THE DOTTED 8TH/16TH NOTE RHYTHM

Like a group of two eighth notes, the dotted eighth/sixteenth note rhythm takes one beat to play; however, unlike evenly played eighth notes, dotted eighth/sixteenths are played unevenly: long short, long short.

Compare the following:

Eighth Notes

Count: 1 & 2 & 3 & 4 & 1 & 2 & 3 & 4 &

Dotted Eighth/Sixteenths

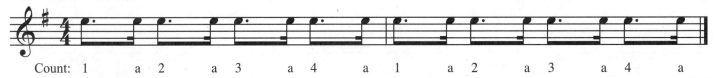

Count: 1   a 2   a 3   a 4   a 1   a 2   a 3   a 4   a

You can think of this rhythm by remembering the sound of the words "humpty dumpty."

Count: hump – ty dump – ty hump – ty dump – ty hump – ty dump – ty hump – ty dump – ty

Toreador Song (from Carmen)

The dotted eighth/sixteenth note rhythm is common in all types of music, such as this example from the world of opera.

Playing hint: When a measure begins with a rest, mark the rest by tapping your foot.

Georges Bizet

Count: 1 & 2 & 3 & 4   1 & 2 & 3   4   1 & 2 & 3   4
        tap   tap   tap

Put Your Little Foot

The dotted eighth/sixteenth note rhythm figures prominently in this country waltz.

Traditional

Shufflin' Along in G

The dotted eighth/sixteenth is the basis for the *shuffle beat* used in rock standards like "Bad, Bad Leroy Brown" and many others. Play this shuffle very rhythmically at a moderate speed.

TEMPO

Tempo is a word of Italian origin used to indicate how fast a piece of music is played. In classical music, tempo indications are usually Italian words. These are only general indications, so taste and ability play important roles in choosing the right tempo. For an exact indication of tempo, metronome markings such as MM=120 are used (see p.4).

Here are the most commonly used tempos with approximate metronome markings. Please note that these are only approximations; your ultimate guide must be your taste and ability. It's far better to sound relaxed and confident at MM=120 than to sound like you're hanging on by your fingernails at MM=160!

Grave (GRAH-veh)	very slow; the slowest tempo used in music	MM=40–48
Largo (LAHR-goh)	slow and broad	MM=48–60
Lento (LEN-toh)	slowly	MM=54–63
Adagio (ah-DAH-joh)	slow, but not as slow as lento	MM=66–76
Andante (ahn-DAHN-teh)	moderately slow; about walking speed	MM=76–104
Allegretto (ahl-leh-GRET-toh)	a little faster than andante	MM=80–100
Moderato (moh-deh-RAH-toh)	moderately fast	MM=108–120
Allegro (ahl-LAY-groh)	fast	MM=124–168
Presto (PRES-toh)	very fast	MM=172–200
Prestissimo (pres-TEES-see-moh)	as fast as possible	MM=over 200

Hint: If you don't have a metronome, you can get a general idea of tempo by imagining yourself marching. That's about 120 beats per minute, or two beats per second. You can also look at the second hand on your watch: MM=60 means 60 beats per minute, or one beat per second.

A few other expressions indicate changes of tempo:

accelerando (aht-chel-le-RAHN-doh), abbreviated *accel.*	getting faster
rallentando (rahl-len-TAHN-doh), abbreviated *rall.*	slowing down
ritardando (ree-tar-DAHN-doh), abbreviated *rit.*	slowing down
stretto (STRET-toh)	hurrying
ad libitum (ahd LEE-bee-toom), abbreviated *ad lib.*	freely, without strict time
rubato (roo-BAH-toh)	somewhat freely
a tempo (ah TEM-poh)	revert to the original tempo

⁶⁄₈ TIME

The 8 in the ⁶⁄₈ time signature means that each eighth note now gets one full beat (unlike in ²⁄₄, ³⁄₄, and ⁴⁄₄, where the quarter note equals one beat). The 6 means that there are six beats per measure. Songs that are played in a slow to moderately slow tempo are counted *in six*, meaning with six full beats per measure.

The next two songs are typical melodies in slow ⁶⁄₈ time. Count them in six.

Drink to Me Only with Thine Eyes

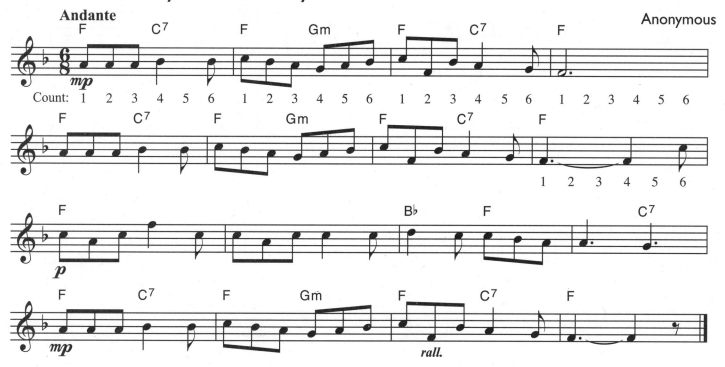

Un Canadien Errant (A Wandering Canadian)

In a fast tempo, $\frac{6}{8}$ time becomes difficult to count in six, so any tempo faster than moderato is counted *in two*. This means that each measure will contain two beats, each beat having the value of a dotted quarter note (three eighth notes).

Count: 1   &   a   2   &   a   1   2   1   2   1   2

The Farmer in the Dell

This familiar children's song is an example of $\frac{6}{8}$ time counted in two.

March   Traditional

The Irish Washerwoman

Brightly   Irish jig

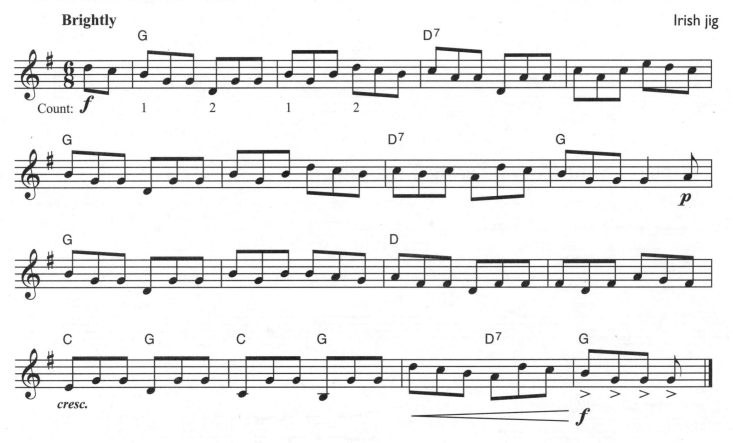

 $\frac{3}{8}$ AND $\frac{9}{8}$ TIME

Each measure of $\frac{3}{8}$ is played like half a measure of $\frac{6}{8}$.

Old Rosin the Bow

Although $\frac{9}{8}$ time is not very common, it has been used in standards such as "The Impossible Dream."
Play each measure as three measures of $\frac{3}{8}$, or as one measure of $\frac{6}{8}$ plus one measure of $\frac{3}{8}$.

Beautiful Dreamer

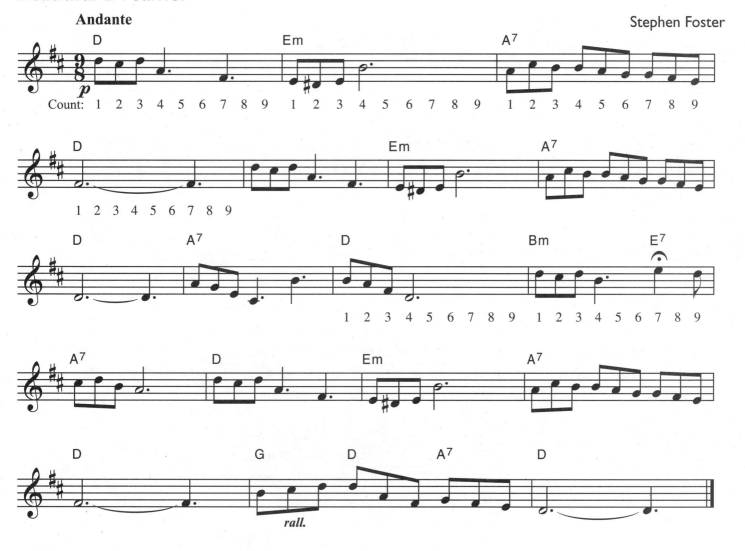

¹²⁄₈ TIME

During the 1950s, ¹²⁄₈ time was often used in so-called *doo-wop* ballads like the later song "I Got You Babe." Play this time as four slow beats to the measure; each beat consists of three eighth notes, or one dotted quarter, or a quarter plus an eighth. You can count *in four*, as if each beat were a triplet.

Doo-Wop Ballad

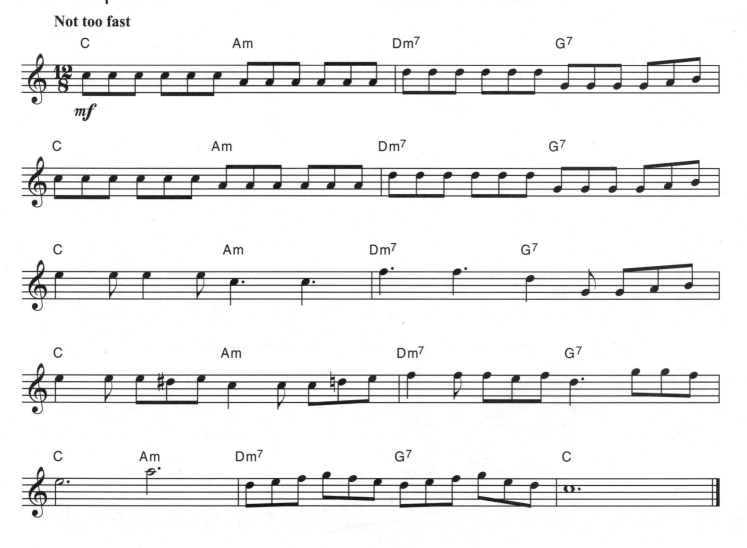

THE DOTTED 8TH/16TH RHYTHM IN $\frac{6}{8}$ TIME

In $\frac{6}{8}$ time, the dotted eighth/sixteenth note rhythm is played like
the dotted quarter/eighth note rhythm in $\frac{4}{4}$, $\frac{3}{4}$ or $\frac{2}{4}$. Count in six.

Greensleeves

Traditional English ballad

The next piece is in a much faster tempo. Start
slowly, counting in six until you get the sound of
the rhythm in your ear. Then, gradually speed up
until you can play in two at about MM=96.

St. Patrick's Day

Irish jig

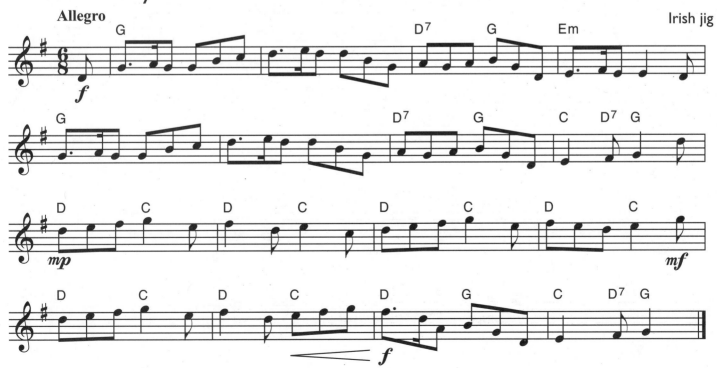

 CUT TIME

The symbol ¢ calls for *cut time*. Cut time looks similar to $\frac{4}{4}$, but is felt as two beats to the measure, with each half note getting one beat. Cut time is used for fast show tunes, marches, and other brightly played music.

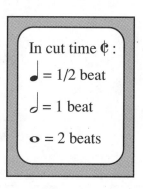

In cut time ¢ :

♩ = 1/2 beat

♩ = 1 beat

𝅝 = 2 beats

The Stars and Stripes Forever

John Philip Sousa

THE QUARTER-NOTE TRIPLET

The *quarter-note triplet* is a group of three quarter notes played in the time of two quarter notes, that is, in two beats. It is rarely seen in meters other than $\frac{4}{4}$ or cut time. This is a very common figure in pop music that many musicians find challenging to play correctly.

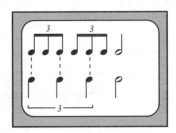

This is one way to learn the quarter-note triplet.

Here is another method of learning the quarter-note triplet.
In the third measure, mentally tie together pairs of notes in the eighth-note triplets.

This example shows the quarter-note triplet used melodically in $\frac{4}{4}$ time.

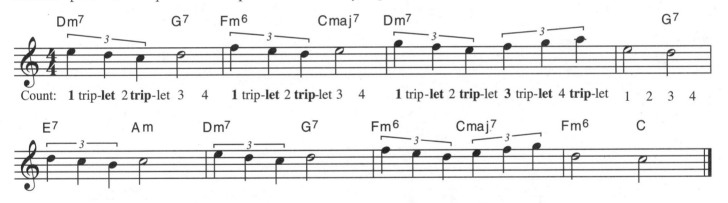

Here are quarter-note triplets used melodically in cut time.
Count them as you would count eighth-note triplets in $\frac{4}{4}$ time.

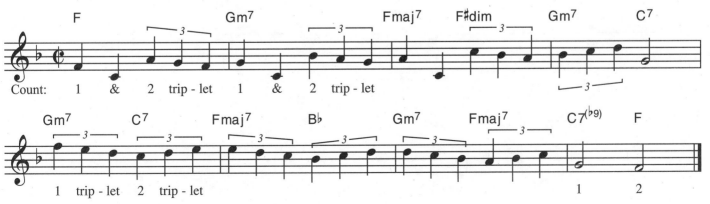

No Quarter Given

Here is a melody in the style of the great show tunes.
Notice the extensive use of the quarter-note triplet.

REPEAT SIGNS

Repeat signs look like double bar lines with two dots. Music between the signs is played twice. (Note: When music repeats from the very beginning of a piece, sometimes the first repeat sign is omitted.) In the line below, the measures are played in the order ①②③④①②③④.

When a different ending is desired for two similar phrases, *1st and 2nd endings* are used. In the next example, play to the repeat sign at the end of measure 8, go back to the beginning, and play everything up to (but not including) the 1st ending. Then, skip the 1st ending and play the 2nd ending instead. The measures are played in the order ①②③④⑤⑥⑦⑧①②③⑤⑥⑨⑩.

Buffalo Gals

Traditional

D.C. al Fine is the abbreviation for *Da Capo al Fine* (dah KAH-poh ahl FEE-neh). It means to repeat from the beginning and play through to the word *Fine*. The following complete version of "Au Claire de la Lune" shows how using repeat signs and D.C. al Fine allows you to write a 16-bar song in only 8 bars. The measures are played in the order ①②③④①②③④⑤⑥⑦⑧①②③④.

Au Claire de la Lune

French folk song

Note: It's not at all unusual to see all the above abbreviations in arrangements, especially in hand-copied manuscripts. Copyists hate to copy the same material twice and often resort to complicated layouts to avoid doing so. This saves them time and trouble, but can make it some what confusing for the player. We suggest always looking over an arrangement to make sure you understand all the repeats, da capos, etc., before attemping to play it.

The expression *D.C. al Coda* stands for the Italian *Da Capo al Coda* (dah KAH-poh ahl KOH-dah). It means to repeat from the beginning, play through to the first *coda sign* ⊕, skip to the second coda sign (toward the end of the piece), and play the measures that follow it. In this variation on "This Old Man," the measures are played in the order ①②③④⑤⑥⑦⑧①②③④⑨⑩⑪⑫.

This Old Man

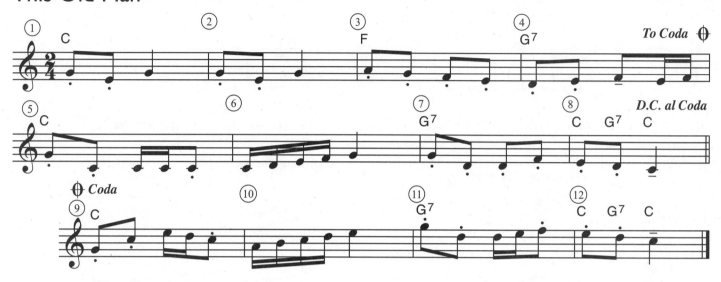

D.S. al Fine stands for *Dal Segno al Fine* (dahl SAY-nyoh ahl FEE-neh). When you see this expression, go back to the *sign* 𝄋 and play through to the word *Fine*. In the following example, the measures are played in the order ①②③④⑤⑥③④.

Hoppin' John

The expression *D.S. al Coda* stands for *Dal Segno al Coda* (dahl SAY-nyoh ahl KOH-dah). When you see this, go back to the sign 𝄋, play from the sign to the first coda sign ⊕, skip to the second coda sign, and complete the piece. In the following example, the measures are played ①②③④⑤⑥⑦⑧③④⑤⑥⑨⑩.

Hansel and Gretel

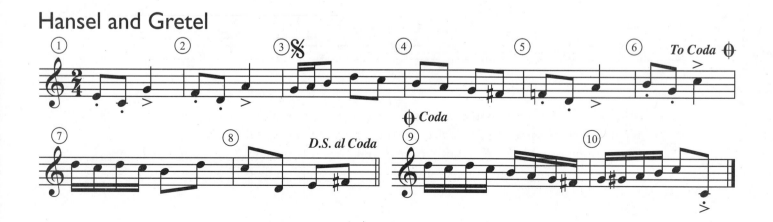

THE KEY OF B♭ MAJOR

The *B♭ major scale* requires B and E to be played as B♭ and E♭. The key signature of two flats is used.

B♭ Major Scale (Lower Octave)

B♭ Major Scale (Upper Octave)

Shift quickly.

This note is high B♭.
It is played on the 1st
string, 6th fret.

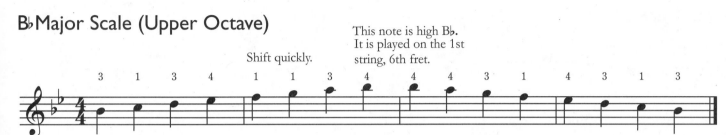

Melody in B♭

A Using the Upper Octave

Moderato

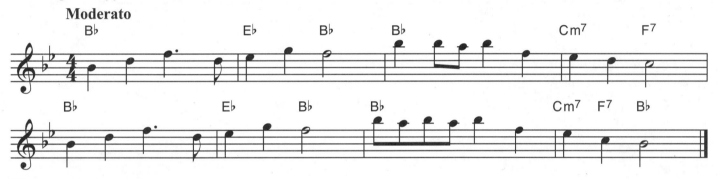

B Using the Lower Octave

Moderato

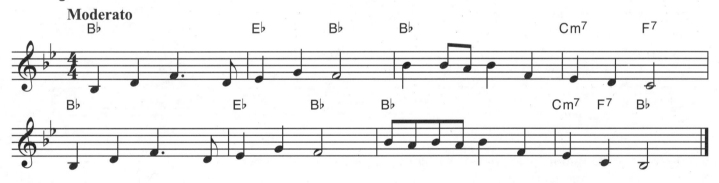

Playing Up the Octave

The guitar is a *transposing* instrument, meaning music for it is written an octave higher than it actually sounds. Because of this, arrangers often notate guitar parts an octave too low, so it isn't unusual for the guitarist to be asked to play a passage an octave higher. The well-rounded musician should be able to do this at sight. For example, if the above melody labeled **B** was marked *8va* or *8va higher*, it would be played exactly the same as the melody labeled **A**.

Guitar Tuning as Written in Treble Clef   Guitar Tuning as It Sounds in Bass Clef

RELATIVE MINOR SCALES

Every major scale has a *relative minor scale* that starts three half steps (three frets) below the major scale. For example, the A minor scale is relative to the C major scale because A is three frets below C.

Each relative minor scale uses the same key signature as its relative major; therefore, the A minor scale uses the same key signature as the C major scale, no sharps or flats.

The easiest minor scale to understand is the *natural minor scale*. Its notes are identical to the notes of the relative major, but it begins and ends on a note three half steps lower.

The scales **G major** and **E minor** are relative to one another. They both use a key signature of one sharp, meaning every F is played as F♯.

The scales **D major** and **B minor** are relative to one an other. They both use a key signature of two sharps, meaning that the F and C are played as F♯ and C♯.

The scales **F major** and **D minor** are relative to one another. They share a key signature of one flat, meaning that every B is played as B♭.

The scales **B♭ major** and **G minor** are relative to one another. They share a key signature of two flats, meaning that B and E are played as B♭ and E♭.

 ## Scale Degrees

The notes of a scale are numbered for easy identification. The numbers are called *scale degrees*. The first degree (number 1) is the *keynote* or *root,* and is the note that names the scale. The other scale tones are numbered in order. Scale tones can also be altered with sharps, flats, or naturals.

HARMONIC MINOR SCALES

Harmonic minor scales are used to construct the basic chords (the *harmony*) in a minor key. They are also used in some types of ethnic music, especially klezmer (Jewish) and some folk songs.

The harmonic minor scale differs from the natural minor scale in that the seventh degree of the harmonic minor is raised a half step.
Compare the following:

A Natural Minor Scale

The 7th degree, G, is unaltered.

A Harmonic Minor Scale

The 7th degree, G, is raised to G♯.

E Natural Minor Scale

The 7th degree, D, is unaltered.

E Harmonic Minor Scale

The 7th degree, D, is raised to D♯.

B Natural Minor Scale

The 7th degree, A, is unaltered.

B Harmonic Minor Scale

The 7th degree, A, is raised to A♯.

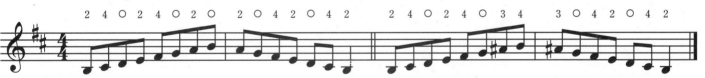

D Natural Minor Scale

The 7th degree, C, is unaltered.

D Harmonic Minor Scale

The 7th degree, C, is raised to C♯.

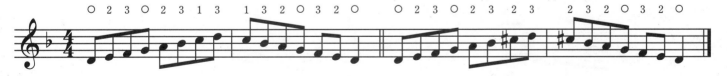

G Natural Minor Scale

The 7th degree, F, is unaltered.

G Harmonic Minor Scale

The 7th degree, F, is raised to F♯.

MELODIC MINOR SCALES

As their name implies, *melodic minor scales* are used to construct melodies. Unlike the natural and harmonic minor scales, the melodic minor is different ascending and descending. When the scale is going up, the 6th and 7th degrees are both raised a half step. When the scale is going down, the 6th and 7th degrees are returned to their unaltered state and played exactly as in the natural minor scale. Compare the following:

A Natural Minor Scale
The 6th and 7th degrees, F and G, are unaltered.

A Melodic Minor Scale
The 6th and 7th degrees, F and G, are raised ascending an unaltered descending.

E Natural Minor Scale
The 6th and 7th degrees, C and D, are unaltered.

E Melodic Minor Scale
The 6th and 7th degrees, C and D, are raised ascending and unaltered descending.

B Natural Minor Scale
The 6th and 7th degrees, G and A, are unaltered.

B Melodic Minor Scale
The 6th and 7th degrees, G and A, are raised ascending and unaltered descending.

D Natural Minor Scale
The 6th and 7th degrees, B♭ and C, are unaltered.

D Melodic Minor Scale
The 6th and 7th degrees, B♭ and C, are raised ascending and unaltered descending.

G Natural Minor Scale
The 6th and 7th degrees, E♭ and F, are unaltered.

G Melodic Minor Scale
The 6th and 7th degrees, E♭ and F, are raised ascending and unaltered descending.

Waltz in A Minor

This waltz is based on the A harmonic minor scale.

Joshua Fit the Battle of Jericho

This famous tune uses the D harmonic minor scale. *To next strain* (bar 8) means to play this measure and then go directly to the next section (**B**).

When you get to *D.C. al Fine*, play the **A** section again, but skip the measure marked *To next strain* and play the *Fine* measure instead. End there.

African-American spritual

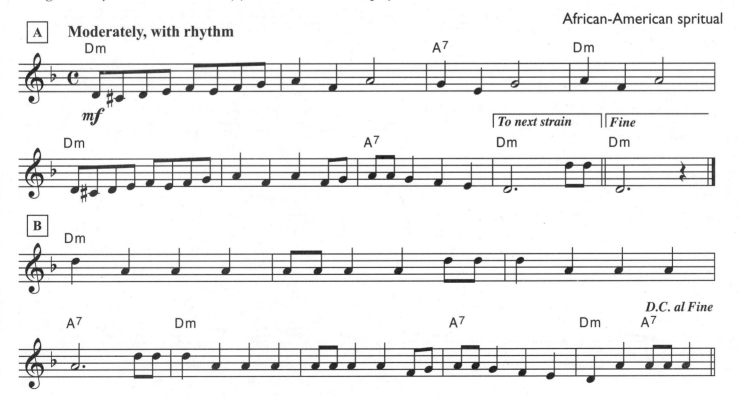

Waves of the Danube

This lovely waltz was written in the 19th century and is the basis for "The Anniversary Song"
heard at many social functions. The melody is based on the A harmonic minor scale,
with measures 18–26 temporarily in the relative key of C major.

Ion Ivanovici

THE KEY OF A MAJOR

The *A major scale* requires F, C, and G to be played as F#, C#, and G#, so the key signature contains these three sharps.

Because the key of A major uses so many open strings, it is often used for pieces intended for the guitar.

A Major Scale (Lower Octave)

A Major Scale (Upper Octave)

Notice that the hand has shifted up one fret so that the 1st finger plays the notes at the fret, the 2nd finger at the 3rd fret, etc.

Two-Octave A Major Scale

This Old Man

Allegretto   Children's song

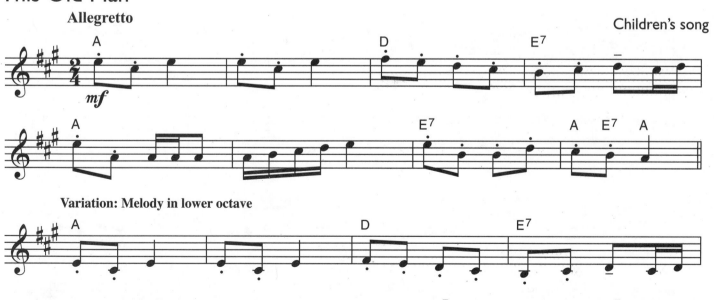

 ## THE SWING FEEL

As you have already learned, eighth notes are played evenly; the upbeat eighth notes are exactly as long as the downbeat eighth notes.

They are counted 1 & 2 &, etc. This is the normal or *straight* feel.

In the *swing* feel, the downbeat eighth notes are slightly longer than the upbeat eighth notes. You can count them as 1 ba 2 ba, or 1 a 2 a, etc. Also, the upbeat eighth notes are slightly accented, exactly the opposite of the straight feel.

(Note that the accent marks are usually not included in the notation. Players are expected to insert them automatically.) The swing feel is sometimes described as being like eighth note triplets with the first two tied together.

Swingin' the Blues in C

The swing feel is sometimes used in country tunes as well as jazz music.

Swingin' In The Country

D-lightful

Swingin' the Blues in A

SYNCOPATION

The word *syncopation* (sink-o-PAY-shun) is defined in *Grove's Dictionary of Music* as "An alteration of the normal time accents of the bar by the setting up of contrary accents." Although this definition is adequate for classical music, it is incomplete with regard to jazz, swing, and other popular styles. The swing feel, which we have already met when playing eighth notes, makes a subtle but crucial difference in the way syncopations are played. Each syncopated note is actually an *anticipation* of a note normally heard on the downbeat. This is a very important rhythmic effect in virtually all kinds of American music, especially jazz, ragtime, rock, rap, and country. It also plays a very important role in Latin-American music, including rhumba, mambo, Afro-Cuban, calypso, Brazilian—virtually every Latin style. So you can see that ability to read syncopation is crucial in developing the ability to read music.

A Short History

Because of the contributions of African-Americans as early as when "Turkey in the Straw" became popular in the mid-1830s, syncopation has played an important part in American music. A few years after the Civil War (certainly by 1885), pianists in St. Louis and other southwestern towns were using an effect in which certain notes were played a little before the downbeat on which they were expected. This was called "ragging the time" or "ragged time," which was soon shortened to *ragtime*. With the publication of huge hits such as "At a Georgia Campmeeting" and "Maple Leaf Rag" in the 1890s, ragtime became a national craze, then an international craze, even influencing classical composers like Igor Stravinsky (*L'Histoire du Soldat*) and Claude Debussy (*Golliwog's Cakewalk*). Other composers such as Darius Milhaud (Dave Brubeck's teacher) and Kurt Weill (*The Threepenny Opera*) continued this tradition into the modern era.

By the 1920s, blues and jazz had replaced ragtime in the public's affection, and great players such as Jellyroll Morton and Earl Hines on piano and Louis Armstrong on trumpet started playing with a more relaxed, flowing rhythm—what we now call the swing feel. Unlike ragtime, which tends to sound a little stiff to modern ears, the music of these masters flows with an easy, swinging feel that still sounds good to us.

The 1930s and '40s saw the rhythms of early jazz incorporated into the big bands of the day. These groups were led by musicians who were either jazz players or had the sense to hire the best jazz talent around, including Duke Ellington, Benny Goodman, Artie Shaw, Count Basie, Tommy and Jimmy Dorsey, Jimmy Lunceford, and a host of others. It was at this time that the demands made on band musicians were increased to include the ability to read complicated syncopations at sight. Even more demanding were the bebop charts that appeared around 1946, which were based on the playing of two of the most talented jazz musicians who ever lived, Charlie Parker (alto sax) and Dizzy Gillespie (trumpet). These arrangements were not only rhythmically complex, but they were also often performed at breakneck tempos, sometimes well over 300 beats per minute!

Since the decline of the big bands after World War II, so-called stage bands have become very popular. There are thousands of young players in high schools and colleges that play the music of today's talented arrangers and composers. Much of this music is written by musicians who have classical training, so it's not unusual to see artificial scales, changes of key and meter, odd meters, dissonant chords, and other techniques associated with modern classical masters such as Béla Bartók, Igor Stravinsky, Paul Hindemith, and Sergei Prokofiev. In other words, the bar keeps being raised, so it behooves the serious musician to develop his or her reading skills to the highest level possible.

Playing Syncopations

As previously mentioned, syncopation is the anticipation of a note that is expected on the downbeat. For example, consider two half notes: the first is played on the downbeat of beat 1 and the second on the downbeat of beat 3.

This figure does not contain any syncopation; however, if we anticipate the second half note by playing it on the "&" of beat 2, we get the following:

This has two important implications:

1. When counting, the next number is 4, not 3, because the anticipated note is on beat 3. This is very important because it's easy to mis-count when playing syncopations.

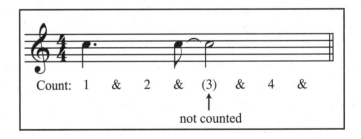

2. Since the anticipated note is a displaced downbeat, all syncopations should be accented. Sometimes arrangers indicate this, other times they take it for granted. In this book, we give you many examples of each. Remember to accent all syncopations, marked or not.

THE ANTICIPATED 3RD BEAT (STRAIGHT FEEL)

The anticipated third beat is, by far, the most commonly seen syncopation in American music. It can be found in jazz, swing, country, rock, rap, hip-hop—virtually every kind of music you might hear today. It is crucial in all forms of Latin-American music as well, including rhumba, salsa, beguine, mambo, etc. Whether playing with a straight feel or swing feel, remember to accent the syncopated note. Make sure you can play the exercises below before attempting the tunes.

Use the straight feel. When played this way, the rhythm is commonly heard in Latin-American music and rock.

These are typical variations of the anticipated third beat.

In these examples, the accent over the syncopated note is understood or taken for granted.

Jamaica Farewell

This well-known calypso tune contains many examples of the anticipated third beat.
Play it with a straight feel.

Caribbean folk song

Rock Bass Line

Play this typical rock bass line from the 1950s and '60s with a straight feel.

Rock Ballad

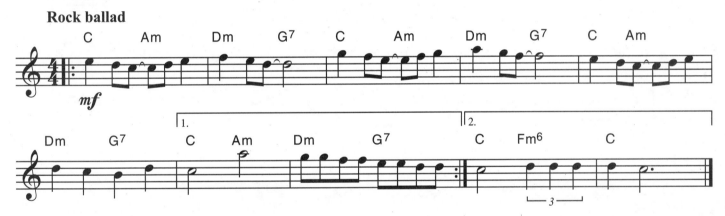

Black and White Rag

The anticipated third beat was also common in early ragtime, as in this excerpt from a tune written in 1909.

THE ANTICIPATED 3RD BEAT (SWING FEEL)

Combining the swing feel with syncopation creates jazz and swing rhythms typically found on lead sheets and in stage band arrangements. (You may want to review the previous section about the swing feel before going on.)

Morty's Tune

Syncopated Swing 1

Nice and easy

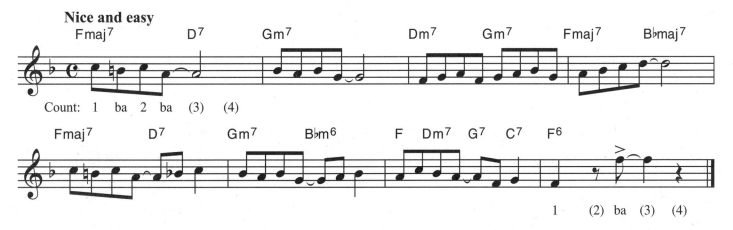

Count: 1 ba 2 ba (3) (4)

1 (2) ba (3) (4)

Syncopated Swing 2

Bright swing feel

Syncopated Swing 3

Medium jazz feel

Second Position

In *second position*, the 1st finger plays the notes at the 2nd fret, the 2nd finger plays the notes at the 3rd fret, the 3rd finger plays the notes at the 4th fret, and the 4th finger plays the notes at the 5th fret. No open strings are used.

Roman numerals are often used to indicate positions. For those of you who slept through that class in school, here are the Roman numerals from 1 to 12:

1	2	3	4	5	6	7	8	9	10	11	12
I	II	III	IV	V	VI	VII	VIII	IX	X	XI	XII

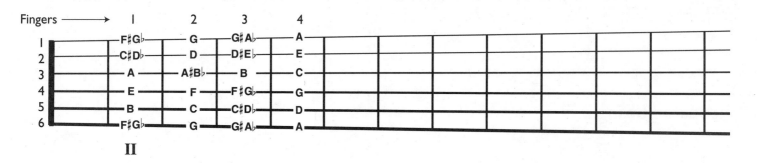

The Notes in Second Position

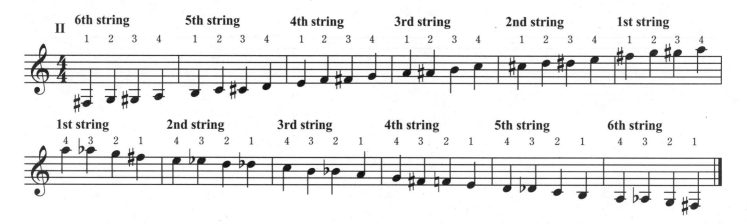

Two-Octave G Major Scale in Second Position

This fingering for the G major scale lies well in the second position. It is very important because it uses no open strings and there-fore can be used all the way up the fingerboard to play a series of major scales. (More about this on later pages.)

INTERVALS

The distance from one note to another is called an *interval*. Starting with the first note as 1, count up the scale to the next note. interval from G to B is called a *third*. Similarly, A to C, B to D, C to E, D to F♯, E to G, and F♯ to A are all thirds.

Study in Thirds

The next-larger interval is called a *fourth*. G to C, A to D, B to E, C to F♯, D to G, E to A, and F♯ to B are all fourths.

Study in Fourths

The next-larger interval is called a *fifth*. In the key of G, the fifths are G to D, A to E, B to F♯, C to G, D to A, E to B, and F♯ to C.

Study in Fifths

Important note: Intervals are determined by letter name only.
For example, G to D, G♯ to D, G♭ to D, G to D♯, G to D♭, G♯ to D♯, etc. are all fifths.
They are different kinds of fifths, and we'll tell you more about this later in the book.

SECOND POSITION, KEY OF D MAJOR

The key of D major also lies well in second position. First practice the scale, then the exercise. After you have a feel for where the notes lie, try the tunes on the next two pages. Remember that the Roman numeral II means to play in second position.

D Major Scale in Second Position

Exercise in Second Position, Key of D Major

Old Aunt Jenny

American country tune

Study in D

This study deals with notes that are not in the scale (accidentals).

Notice how the 1st finger dips down out of 2nd position.

A Condo in Aruba

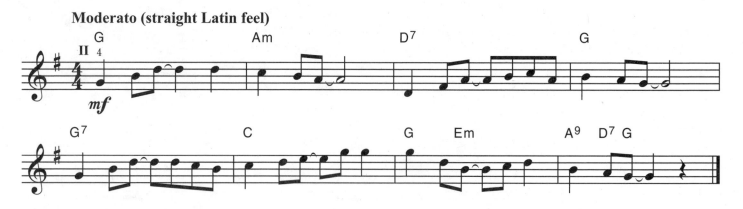

A Condo in Aruba (Variation)

This is a variation of the tune above. Be sure to mark each initial rest with a foot tap.

Chasin' the Charleston

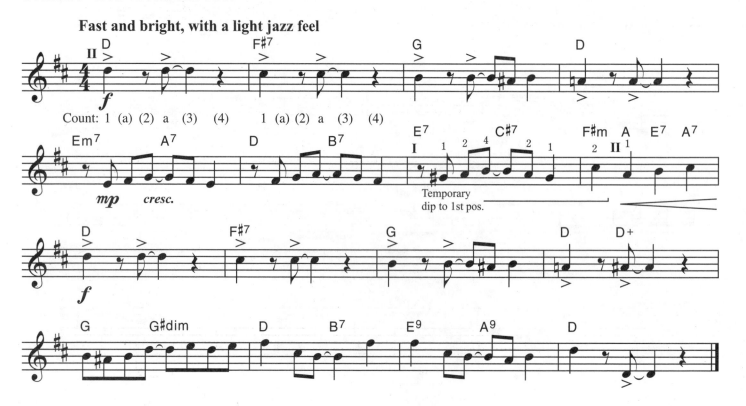

THE ANTICIPATED 2ND BEAT (STRAIGHT FEEL)

The anticipated second beat, also known as the eighth/quarter/eighth rhythm, is very common in all types of music. The folk song "Tom Dooley" starts with this rhythm, as does "Rudolph, the Red-Nosed Reindeer."

Usually the second note is cut off short. In the example below, measure 1 is often played to sound like measure 2.

Count: 1   &   2   &   3   4   1   &   2   &   3   4

Learn these four measures, then try playing "Tom Dooley."

Count: 1   &   (2)   &   3   (4)   1   &   (2)   &   3   (4)   1   &   (2)   &   3   4   1   &   (2)   &   3   (4)

Tom Dooley (with Variations)

Play the tune in either first or second position. Variation 1 develops the anticipated 2nd beat with other rhythms. The second variation combines the anticipated 2nd beat in one measure with the anticipated 3rd beat in another.

THE ANTICIPATED 2ND BEAT (SWING FEEL)

The anticipated 2nd beat is cut off rather short in the swing feel as well as in the straight feel.
You can remember this by using the nonsense syllables "da bop ba da."

Swing feel

Count: 1 Bop (2) ba Da   (4)   1 Bop (2) ba Da   (4)   1 Bop (2) ba 3   4   1 Bop (2) ba Da   (4)

Bebop

Play this bebop line in second position.

Jazz Waltz

The anticipated 2nd beat appears in ¾ time, especially in jazz waltzes.
Play this one in first position with a solid swing feel.

Third Position

In *third position*, the 1st finger plays the notes at the 3rd fret, the 2nd finger plays the notes at the 4th fret, the 3rd finger plays the notes at the 5th fret, and the 4th finger plays the notes at the 6th fret. The Roman numeral for this position is III.

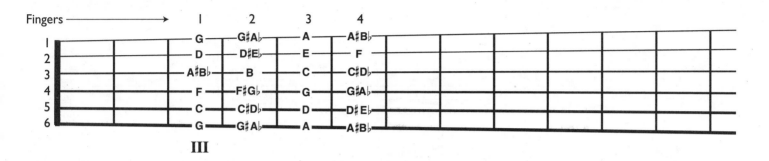

The Notes in Third Position

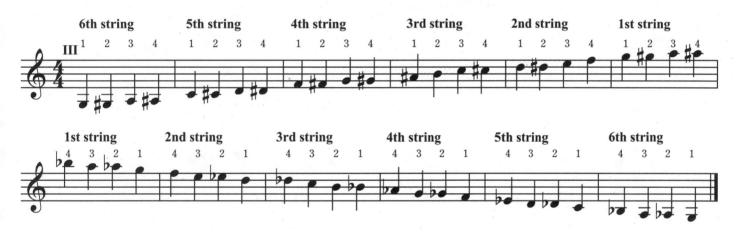

Two-Octave A♭ Major Scale in Third Position

One of the big advantages to playing in position is that the fingering for each scale remains the same as you move up the fingerboard. The two-octave A♭ major scale in third position is fingered exactly the same as the two-octave G major scale in second position, except that the hand has moved one fret higher.

THIRD POSITION, KEY OF A♭ MAJOR

Scale Study in A♭

Study in Thirds

Study in Fourths

THIRD POSITION, KEY OF E♭ MAJOR

The *E♭ major scale* requires the notes B, E, and A to be played flat.
The *key of E♭ major* lies well in third position. First practice the scale, then the exercises.
After you have a feel for where the notes lie, try the tunes on the next two pages.

E♭ Major Scale in Third Position

Exercises in Third Position, Key of E♭ Major

CHANGING POSITIONS

The following is an exercise by the famous violin teacher Rudolphe Kreutzer. It is an excellent example of how changing positions in the middle of a piece helps to keep the fingering logical. Because the basic key is E♭, most of the piece is played in third position, but second and first positions are also used. Notice how open strings are used to change positions whenever possible. This gives you a fraction of a second longer to do a smooth shift.

SYNCOPATION IN THIRD POSITION

Here is a typical figure used in early rock music. Play with a straight feel.

Boppin' in Hollywood

The opening figure of the next tune is nothing more than the eighth/quarter/eighth figure, but with a rest in place of the first eighth note. Tap your foot for the rest and this shouldn't give you any trouble.

THE ANTICIPATED 4TH BEAT

This figure should give you little trouble, because it is very similar to the anticipated 2nd beat. The same eighth/quarter/eighth now appears as the second half of a $\frac{4}{4}$ measure.

The quarter note is usually cut off short, so the first and second measures of the examples below are played nearly the same.

Here are some other examples of the anticipated 4th beat.

Don't forget to tap for initial rests.

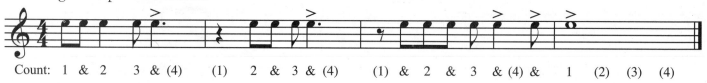

It's often been said that rests are harder to play than notes. Count carefully.

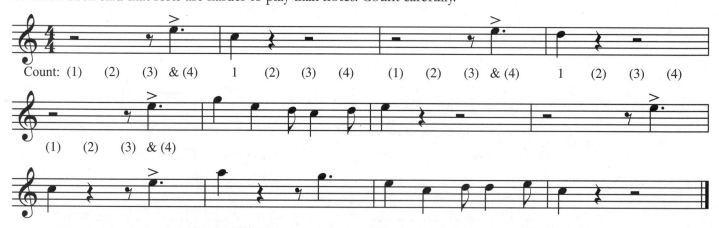

This example combines the anticipated 4th beat with triplets.

Penthouse in Paris

The anticipated 4th beat often occurs in measures along with the anticipated 2nd beat.

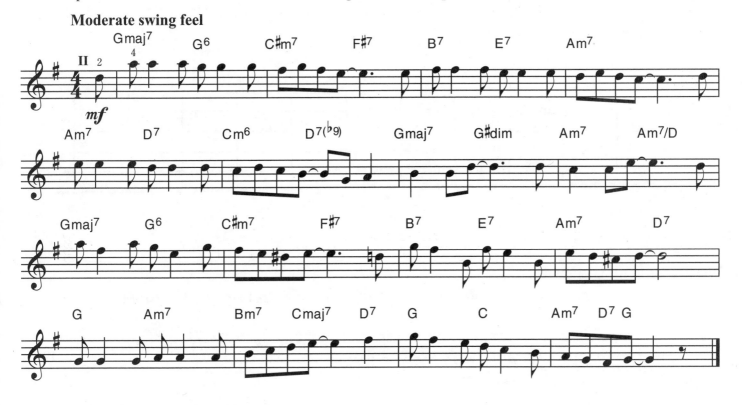

Chi-Chi Cha-Cha

The *cha-cha* (or, more properly, the "cha-cha-cha") is a popular Latin-American dance played with a straight feel at about 120 beats per minute. This example is in the third position.

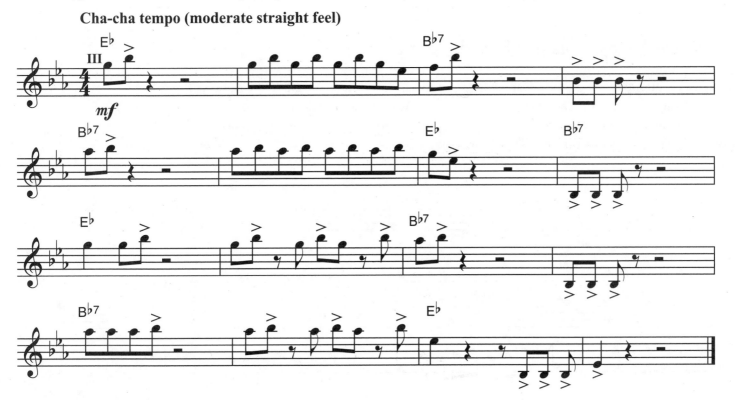

Fourth Position

In the *fourth position*, the 1st finger plays the notes at the 4th fret, the 2nd finger plays the notes at the 5th fret, the 3rd finger plays the notes at the 6th fret, and the 4th finger plays the notes at the 7th fret. The Roman number for this position is IV.

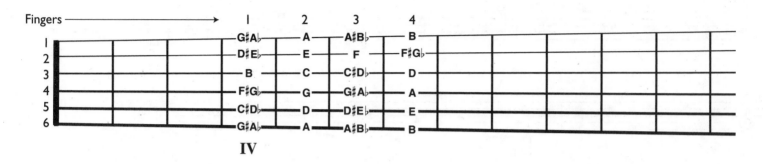

The Notes in Fourth Position

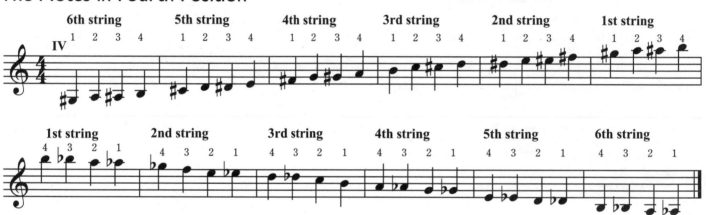

Two-Octave A Major Scale in Fourth Position

As we have mentioned, one of the advantages to playing in position is that the fingering for each scale remains the same as you move up the fingerboard. The two-octave A major scale in fourth position is fingered exactly the same as the two-octave A♭ major scale in third position, except that the hand has moved one fret higher.

Fourth Position, Key of A Major

Scale Study in A

Study in Thirds

Study in Fourths

FOURTH POSITION, KEY OF E MAJOR

The *E major scale* requires four notes to be sharped: F♯, C♯, G♯, and D♯. The *key of E major* is a favorite among folk, country, and rock guitar players be- cause the chords are the fullest and richest sounding on the instrument. Playing single-string figures in the key of E is comfortable in fourth position.

E Major Scale in Fourth Position

Scale Study in E

Jimmy Crack Corn

American folk song

GRACE NOTES

A *grace note* is a small-sized note that precedes a melody note. Grace notes are played very quickly, just before the melody note. When the grace note is be- low the melody note, you can either slide up to the melody note with the same finger or hammer-on to the melody note with the next finger higher.

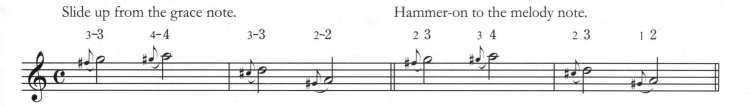

To play grace notes from above, you can slide down from the grace note to the melody note with the same finger, or you can pull-off from the grace note to the melody note.

Ja-Da

This tune uses grace notes with an easy swing feel.

Bob Carleton

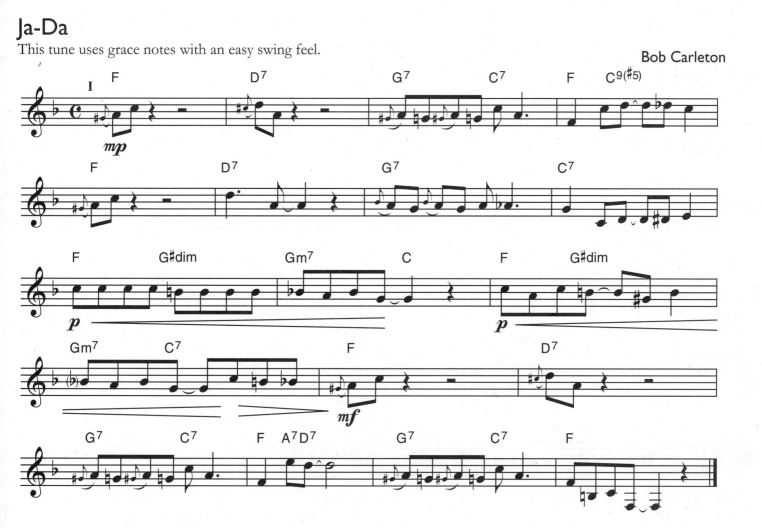

TRIPLETS AND ANTICIPATED BEATS

A common figure you'll see in ballads and other music at slow tempos has the last note of an eighth-note triplet tied to the next note.

Again, the tied note should always be accented because it is actually the anticipation of the next beat.

Count: 1 trip-let 2 trip-let 3 (4)   1 trip-let 2 trip-let (3) (4)   1 trip-let 2 trip-let (3) 4   1(trip)let 2 trip-let (3) (4)

A Walk in the Park

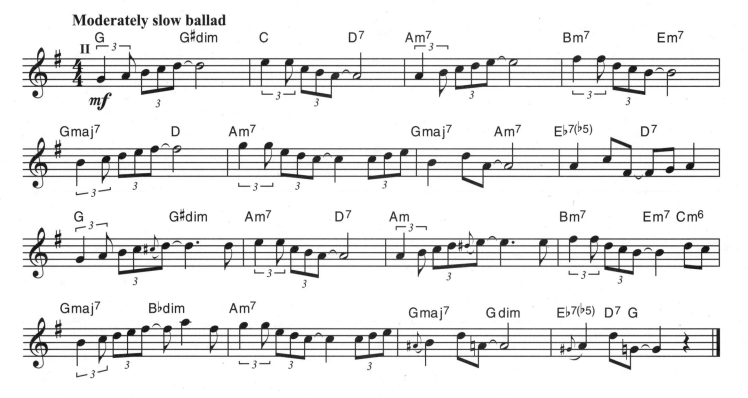

Strollin'

Although less common, the 2nd and 4th beats may also be anticipated with a triplet.

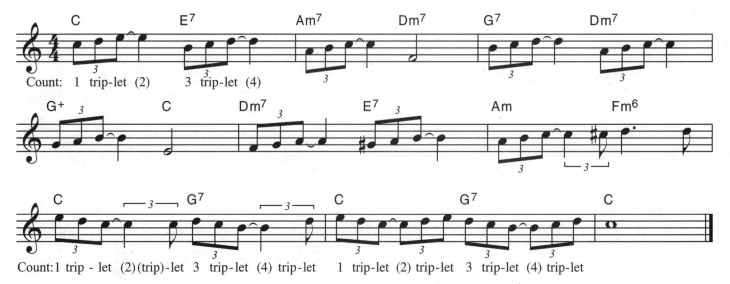

Count: 1 trip-let (2)   3 trip-let (4)

Count:1 trip - let (2)(trip)-let 3 trip-let (4) trip-let   1 trip-let (2) trip-let 3 trip-let (4) trip-let

THE ANTICIPATED 1ST BEAT

The anticipated 1st beat is the single most difficult syncopation to play correctly because the anticipated note appears in the previous measure. In the first ex-

ample below, the last note of measure 1 is actually the anticipated first beat of measure 2. This rhythm is very common, and it is extremely important to master.

Straight feel

Swing feel

Practice these melodic examples of the same rhythm with both the straight and the swing feel.

The St. Louis Blues

This modern arrangement of a blues classic features a lot of syncopation including the anticipated 1st beat as well as grace notes and playing in second position.

Fifth Position

In *fifth position*, the 1st finger plays the notes at the 5th fret, the 2nd finger plays the notes at the 6th fret, the 3rd finger plays the notes at the 7th fret, and the 4th finger plays the notes at the 8th fret.

The Roman number for this position is V. Fifth position is especially important on the guitar because it's used for the keys of F and B♭, two very common keys in all kinds of jazz and Latin styles.

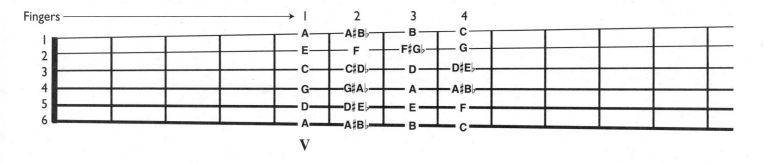

The Notes in Fifth Position

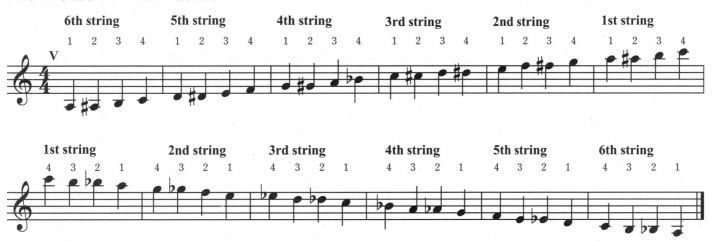

Two-Octave B♭ Major Scale in Fifth Position

The two-octave B♭ major scale in fifth position is fingered exactly the same as the two-octave A major scale in fourth position, except the hand has moved one fret higher.

FIFTH POSITION, KEY OF B♭ MAJOR

Scale Study in B♭

Study in Fifth Position

Listen to the Mockingbird

Here's a little something for all you fans of the "Three Stooges." It's a jazzed up version
of a pop song from the 1800s that the nutty trio used as a theme song.
Play it in the fifth position with a straight feel.

Winner and Milburn

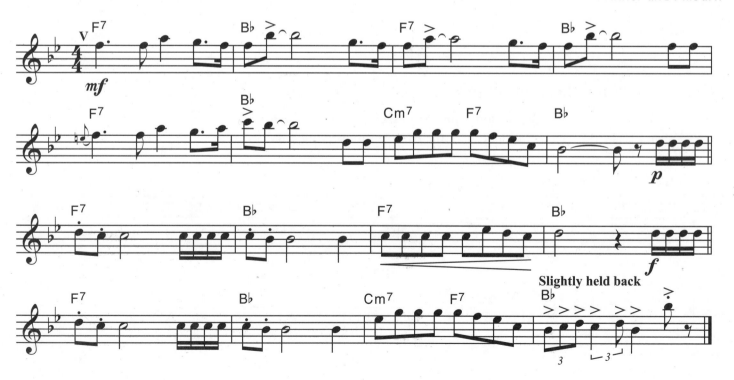

FIFTH POSITION, KEY OF F MAJOR

The key of F major lies well in fifth position. It uses the same fingering as the key of D in second position, the key of E♭ in third position, and the key of E in fourth position. First practice the scale, then play the tunes.

F Major Scale in Fifth Position

This next study features the interval of a *sixth*. The sixths in the key of F are F to D, G to E, A to F, B♭ to G, C to A, D to B♭, and E to C.

Study with Sixths

Waltz in F

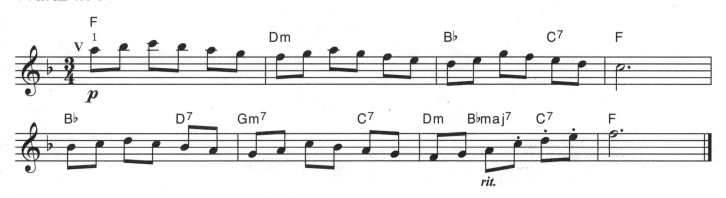

RHYTHM AND POSITION REVIEW

This page reviews the anticipated 1st, 2nd, 3rd, and 4th beats (but never more than one per measure). The second, third, fourth, and fifth positions also get a workout. Notice that changes of key signature are indicated both at the end of the staff and at the beginning of the new staff.

Note: The so-called "hat" accent ∧ is a shorter, sharper accent than >.

TWO SYNCOPATIONS PER MEASURE

Anticipated 2nd and 4th Beats

Count: 1   & (2) &   3   & (4) &   1   2   3   4   1   bop (2) ba   3 bop (4) ba   1   2   3   4

Anticipated 2nd and 4th Beats in G

Anticipated 2nd and 4th Beats with Other Syncopations

Anticipated 2nd and 3rd Beats

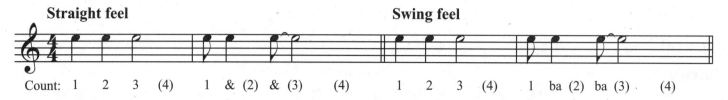

Count: 1 2 3 (4) 1 & (2) & (3) (4) 1 2 3 (4) 1 ba (2) ba (3) . (4)

Anticipated 2nd and 3rd Beats in F

Anticipated 3rd and 4th Beats

Count: 1 2 3 4 1 (&) (2) & (3) & (4) (&) 1 2 3 4 1 (ba) (2) ba (3) ba (4) (ba)

Anticipated 3rd and 4th Beats in C

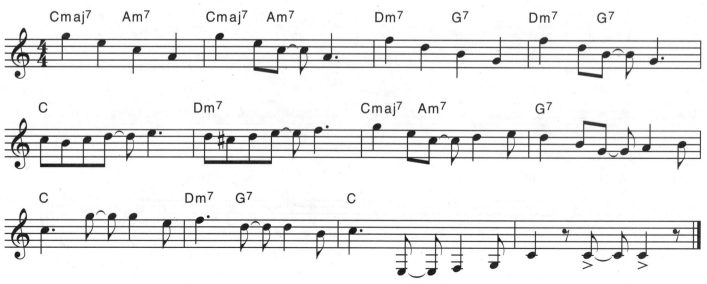

As previously mentioned, the anticipated 1st beat is the trickiest one to play correctly.

This page consists of short examples of the anticipated 1st beat combined with various other syncopations.

Anticipated 1st Beat with Other Syncopations

Jazz Ballad

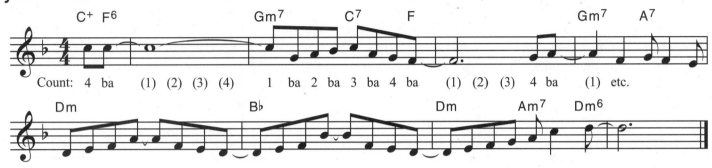

Shortnin' Bread Rock

Relaxed Rock

Sixth Position

In *sixth position*, the 1st finger plays the notes at the 6th fret, the 2nd finger plays the notes at the 7th fret, the 3rd finger plays the notes at the 8th fret, and the 4th finger plays the notes at the 9th fret. Because this position is well-suited to the rarely used keys of B major (five sharps) and F♯ major (six sharps), we won't go into it in detail. We urge you, however, to replay pages 96 and 97 as follows: For examples that are in the key of B♭, mentally change the key signature to five sharps (F♯, C♯, G♯, D♯, and A♯) and play one fret higher in sixth position. For examples that are in the key of F, mentally change the key signature to six sharps (F♯, C♯, G♯, D♯, A♯, and E♯) and play one fret higher in sixth position.

Seventh Position

In *seventh position*, the 1st finger plays the notes at the 7th fret, the 2nd finger plays the notes at the 8th fret, the 3rd finger plays the notes at the 9th fret, and the 4th finger plays the notes at the 10th fret. The Roman numeral for this position is VII. Seventh position is especially important for the guitar because it's used for the keys of C and G, two very common keys in all kinds of styles.

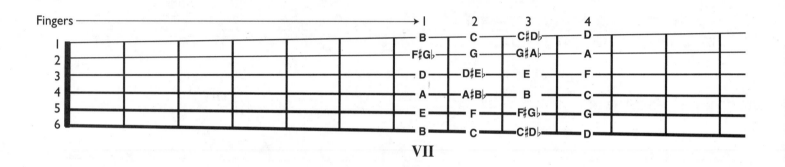

The Notes in Seventh Position

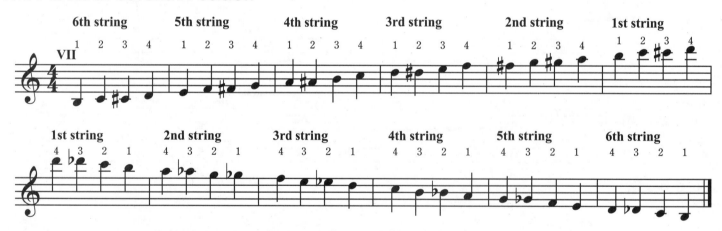

Two-Octave C Major Scale in Seventh Position

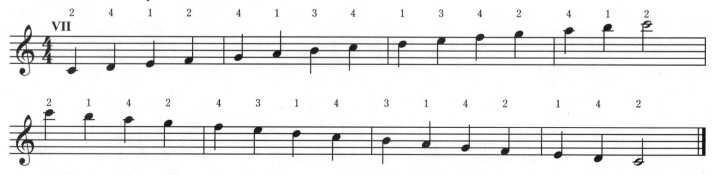

SEVENTH POSITION, KEY OF C MAJOR

Scale Study in Seventh Position

Study in Seventh Position

Little Waltz in C

SEVENTH POSITION, KEY OF G MAJOR

The key of G major lies well in seventh position. It uses the same fingering as the key of D in second position, the key of E♭ in third position, and the key of F in fifth position. First practice the scale, then play the tunes.

G Major Scale in Seventh Position

Study with Sevenths in Seventh Position

This next study features the interval of a *seventh*. The sevenths in the key of G are G to F♯, A to G, B to A, C to B, D to C, E to D, and F♯ to E.

Arietta (Opening Theme)

Franz Joseph Haydn

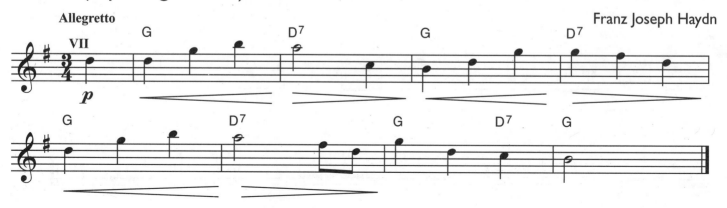

SYNCOPATION IN SEVENTH POSITION

The Old Soft Shoe

Poco a poco means "little by little."

A Touch of Salsa

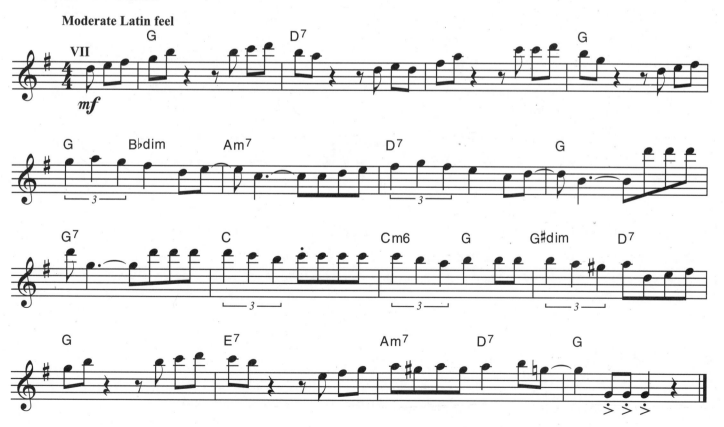

DOUBLE TIME

Starting in the 1960s, a new rhythmic feel entered American rock music known as the *double time* feel. Instead of the basic pulse being the quarter note, the basic rhythm is the eighth note, thus the name "double time." Typical examples of this feel are "Let It Be" by the Beatles or "Stayin' Alive" by the BeeGees. The swing feel is almost never used, so practice all the examples with a straight feel.

First, review some examples in double time.

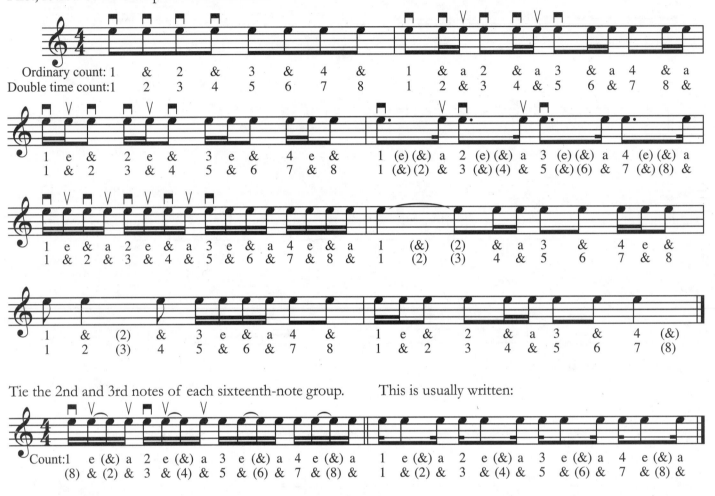

Tie the 2nd and 3rd notes of each sixteenth-note group.　　This is usually written:

Double time syncopations involve anticipated eighth notes.

Anticipated 3rd and 7th Eighth Notes

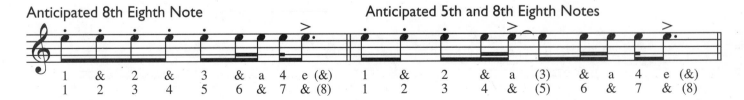

Anticipated 8th Eighth Note　　Anticipated 5th and 8th Eighth Notes

Anticipated 1st Eighth Note

The following are some examples of the double time feel used melodically.

Disco Beat

Rock Ballad

Funk

Tango

Tangos are often written with a double time feel in $\frac{2}{4}$ time, as in this example.

FIRST POSITION, KEY OF D♭ MAJOR

The *key of D♭* has five flats: B♭, E♭, A♭, D♭, and G♭. No need to be intimidated, however; the fingering is the same as for the key of D in second position, but one fret lower in first position. If you're serious about reading music, you should master this scale and key, as it has been used for many jazz standards including "Stompin' at the Savoy," "Body and Soul," and "Lush Life," to name just a few.

D♭ Major Scale in First Position

Study in D♭

ODD METERS

An *odd meter* is a meter that cannot be broken down into equal groups of beats. The general rule for odd meters is to break them down into smaller groups of two, three, or four beats. For example, $\frac{5}{4}$ (made famous by Dave Brubeck in his jazz standard "Take Five") can be thought of as a measure of $\frac{3}{4}$ plus a measure of $\frac{2}{4}$; music in $\frac{7}{4}$ is usually played as a measure of $\frac{3}{4}$ plus a measure of $\frac{4}{4}$. A measure of $\frac{7}{8}$ (very common in Greek music) can be thought of as a measure of $\frac{3}{8}$ plus a measure of $\frac{2}{4}$ ($\frac{4}{8}$). Often, the way the notes are connected with beams indicates how to break down the measure.

The following example shows $\frac{5}{4}$ broken down as $\frac{3}{4}$ plus $\frac{2}{4}$.

Homage to D.B.

Greek Dance No. 1

Greek Dance No. 2

SYNCOPATED ACCENTS

By placing accents on off-beats, a syncopated effect can be obtained that has been very common since the early days of ragtime right up to, and includ-ing, rap and hip-hop. Play this famous ragtime tune with a swing feel and make sure to bring out the accented notes.

12th Street Rag

E. L. Bowman

WHERE TO GO FROM HERE

If you've mastered all the information in this book...congratulations! You are able to read at sight virtually any lead sheet or stage band arrangement you come across. This gives you an enormous advantage over the great majority of guitarists who can only read a chord sheet, if that.

If you aspire to be a competent professional—and by that we means someone who can handle virtually any type of music that gets thrown at you—you will want to continue your studies.

Dan Fox's *Rhythm Bible* (also published by Alfred) takes up syncopation in greater detail than this book. If you can play through the *Rhythm Bible*, it's unlikely that you'll run across something you've never seen before or can't figure out.

If you're particularly interested in avant garde jazz, find books that specialize in odd meters and exotic scales.

As you know, this book only takes you up to seventh position. Although this is high enough for most situations, we suggest using violin books such as the Sitt position studies to learn the extreme higher positions. Most modern guitars go up to at least a double high C or even higher, and there is a real dearth of good material that will teach you to read in these registers.

Another suggestion for those who enjoy a challenge is to obtain the four books of clarinet exercises by Fritz Kroepsch. Since the clarinet has the identical range as the guitar, (low E to double high C) these books will train you to play all over the guitar's range. The rhythms are not difficult, but the notes are challenging enough for the most demanding professional.

Although playing in positions is an efficient way to sight-read, it's not always the best way to play any particular passage. Learning where to play some-

thing on the guitar is a challenge that can only be overcome by a lifetime of study and experience.

Finally, reading music is like any other skill: it requires practice. We suggest that you obtain many different types of music. Read them using a metronome. Try not to memorize, but to look at each page with a fresh eye. Start with fake books, such as those listed below. These collections of hundreds of songs in lead sheet (single line) form will present you with many rhythmic and melodic problems in a variety of meters and keys. Collections of trumpet, clarinet, or saxophone studies or jazz solos all can be played on the guitar. These will give you practical experience in playing syncopations. So remember the three rules of learning to read music fluently:
1. Read 2. Read 3. Read!

Good luck with your career.
Dan Fox

Suggested Fake Books from Alfred Publishing

Just Blues Real Book 00-FBM0004
Just Classic Rock Real Book 00-FBM0005
Just Jazz Real Book 00-FBM0003
Just Standards Real Book 00-FBM0002
The World's Greatest Fakebook 00-F3287FBC

Guitar Fingerboard Chart
Frets 1–12

STRINGS

Fret	6th	5th	4th	3rd	2nd	1st
Open	E	A	D	G	B	E
1st Fret	F	A#/B♭	D#/E♭	G#/A♭	C	F
2nd Fret	F#/G♭	B	E	A	C#/D♭	F#/G♭
3rd Fret	G	C	F	A#/B♭	D	G
4th Fret	G#/A♭	C#/D♭	F#/G♭	B	D#/E♭	G#/A♭
5th Fret	A	D	G	C	E	A
6th Fret	A#/B♭	D#/E♭	G#/A♭	C#/D♭	F	A#/B♭
7th Fret	B	E	A	D	F#/G♭	B
8th Fret	C	F	A#/B♭	D#/E♭	G	C
9th Fret	C#/D♭	F#/G♭	B	E	G#/A♭	C#/D♭
10th Fret	D	G	C	F	A	D
11th Fret	D#/E♭	G#/A♭	C#/D♭	F#/G♭	A#/B♭	D#/E♭
12th Fret	E	A	D	G	B	E